CW01010988

Thistledown Farm:
Farmer John's Boots
and
Other Stories

David C Evans

Illustrated by Jake Tebbit

Pen Press

© David C Evans 2010

All rights reserved

No part of this publication may be reproduced, stored in a retrieval system, or transmitted in any form or by any means, without the prior permission in writing of the publisher, nor be otherwise circulated in any form of binding or cover other than that in which it is published and without a similar condition including this condition being imposed on the subsequent purchaser.

First published in Great Britain by Pen Press

All paper used in the printing of this book has been made from wood grown in managed, sustainable forests.

ISBN13: 978-1-907172-31-1

Printed and bound in the UK
Pen Press is an imprint of Indepenpress Publishing Limited
25 Eastern Place
Brighton
BN2 1GJ

A catalogue record of this book is available from the British Library

Cover design by Jake Tebbit

'The Champion Dung Spreader' words and music by Adge Cutler.
© 1967 reproduced by permission of Ardmoore & Beechwood Ltd and EMI Music Publishing, London, W8 5SW

Illustrations © Jake Tebbit 2009

For all my friends and family

Acknowledgements to Alison Hunt for her support and superb secretarial skills.

About the Author

 David Charles Evans BSc.(Hons) was born in Nakuru, Kenya into an old farming family, his grandparents being Kenya pioneers from Shropshire, and was brought up on the family farm in West Devon.

He studied agriculture at Seale-Hayne College, Newton Abbot and spent his time pedigree sheep breeding and sheep shearing before settling in Exeter and developing his ideas for a humorous children's character based upon the eccentricities of all the farmers he has known and Farmer John Stubblefield was born. David is currently an active member of Exeter Writers and has many more Farmer John stories up his sleeve.

Contact David at www.farmerjohnsboots.co.uk

About the Illustrator

Jake Tebbit has been an illustrator for all his working life.

He trained as a graphic designer at Kingston School of Art and worked first as a background artist at Halas & Batchelor, the British Animation Company, then moved on to become Senior Editorial Artist for Reed Publishing, before going Freelance in 1977.

He has worked with many publishers of Children's story books, Educational text books, Agricultural and reference books and his pictures have been used to illustrate several of the BBC's Jackanory programmes.

In his spare time he teaches Illustration to students at a local Sixth Form College and is well known for his 'jolly' cartoons, which can be viewed on his website: www.jaketebbit.co.uk

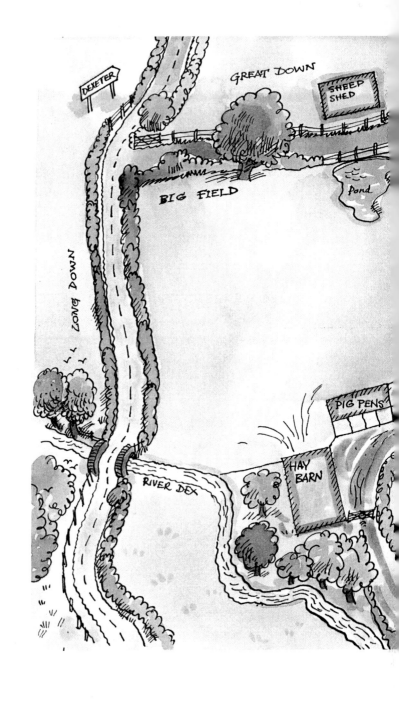

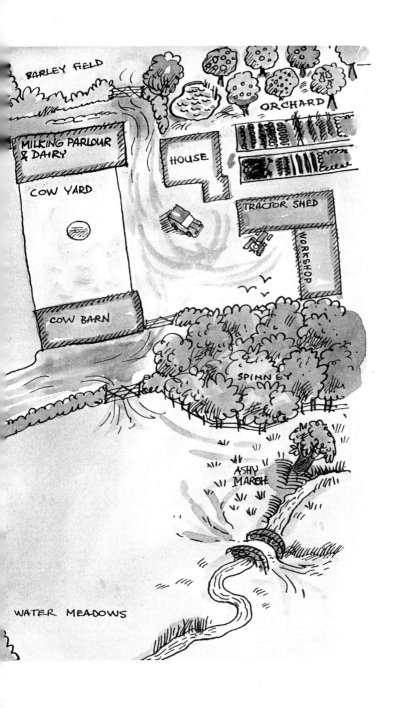

Contents

FARMER JOHN'S BOOTS

**Farmer John's boots go missing, but PC Collar
is soon on the trail…**

One *dark* winter morning Farmer John crawled out of bed and groped for his clothes. Wendy his wife was still asleep. He didn't want to wake her. At last he managed to get dressed and tiptoed downstairs to go milking.

In the porch he turned on the light and looked for his wellingtons. There were his shoes and his trainers and his slippers but the space where his wellingtons usually were was empty!

'Where on earth have my wellingtons gone?' said Farmer John, annoyed. 'I've got work to do and I can't go outside in my bare feet.' He rummaged through the junk in the cupboard but they weren't there. 'How am I expected to milk the cows without any boots?' he complained. 'Oh well, the cows won't wait, I'll have to make do.'

He got two plastic bin bags from the kitchen, tied them over his shoes then went out into the y The cows laughed when they saw him coming. 'I HA,' they chuckled, 'we know you're short of John, but can't you even afford a pair of bo

Farmer John grunted. 'Huh,' he said. 'My wellingtons have disappeared. I can't find them anywhere, it's not funny.'

The cows giggled, 'But boots don't just vanish into thin air, John, unless they're magic boots, of course.'

Farmer John snorted. 'Magic boots indeed, whoever heard of such a thing!'

The cows had a great laugh making fun of Farmer John's bin bag gumboots and by the time he had finished milking Farmer John was quite fed up. 'I've had enough of this,' he said. 'I'm going to have my breakfast.'

Wendy was in the kitchen when he came in.

'Goodness' said Wendy, 'you're wearing bin bags! What's happened to your boots?'

'They've gone missing,' said Farmer John.

'Really?' said Wendy, 'that's odd. Have you looked?'

'YES,' said Farmer John, 'when I came down this morning they weren't in the porch.'

'How strange!' said Wendy 'Perhaps they're hiding.'

'What do you mean *hiding*?' said Farmer John crossly. 'Boots don't have a mind of their own! Just give me my breakfast, will you?'

Wendy ignored him. 'Perhaps they've been stolen!' she said.

'Stolen!' cried Farmer John. 'Who would want to steal my boots?'

'I don't know,' shrugged Wendy. 'Maybe a thief.'

'Hmm…That's possible,' said Farmer John. 'Perhaps I ought to call the police.'

So Farmer John called the police. PC Collar turned up in the farmyard in his smart police car. He squeezed himself out.

'Morning John,' he said. 'What's the problem?'

'I've lost my boots,' said Farmer John. 'They've been stolen!'

'Really?' said PC Collar. 'I've never heard of boots being stolen before, are you sure they haven't walked off on their own?'

Farmer John was not amused. 'I don't think you're taking this seriously enough,' he said. 'I expected better of the police force!'

'Now, now, John,' soothed the policeman. 'I'm sure there's a logical explanation. Perhaps you could give me a description?'

'Well,' said Farmer John, 'they're green.'

'Size?' asked PC Collar.

'Ten,' said Farmer John.

'Any distinguishing marks?'

'They've got quite a lot of muck on them,' said Farmer John.

'Hmm,' pondered the policeman. 'What does the tread look like?'

Farmer John drew him a picture.

'Let me see,' said PC Collar. 'I might be able to track them down.' He got out a magnifying glass and looked at the ground. 'Here we are,' he said, and in the mud of the farmyard was a *large* footprint.

PC Collar began to follow the trail of footprints. He carefully walked around the yard down to the pig-pens. There was a mess of prints by the pig-pen wall. Then he followed them past the barn to the cow yard.

'That must be where I fed the cows yesterday,' said Farmer John. 'It's a good job I didn't clean the yards or I wouldn't have left any marks.'

The policeman grunted. 'You certainly seem to get around all over the place on *this* farm,' he said, and carried on following the footprints.

They went from the cow yard to the sheep shed…

…from the sheep shed to the workshop…

…from the workshop to the tractor shed…

…from the tractor shed to the garden...

…and from the garden back to the farmhouse!

PC Collar scratched his head. 'Well, by my reckoning,' he said, 'they should be in the house.' He bent down and looked at the floor; there was a *big* mucky footprint on the carpet. The policeman bent over with his magnifying glass.

'It's your boots,' he said and he began to follow them into the house.

They went through the hall…

…up the stairs…

…along the landing...

…and into Farmer John's bedroom.

They went round the bed...

…and there, on Farmer John's side, was a pair of mucky green wellingtons!

The policeman held them up at arm's length. 'Are these *yours,* sir?' He said, wrinkling his nose.

Farmer John blushed. 'Of course, *now* I remember. I was *so tired* last night I couldn't be bothered to take them off in the porch. I just came straight upstairs in my wellies and flopped into bed!'

PC Collar laughed. 'Well,' he said, 'that's one mystery solved but in future I'd advise you to take your wellingtons off downstairs, it would save a lot of police time!'

Wendy was a bit cross when she discovered that Farmer John had left his mucky boots in their bedroom but she soon forgave him, and all the animals hooted with laughter when they heard how the mystery of Farmer John's missing boots had been solved!

FARMER JOHN'S VALENTINE

Everyone gets a Valentine's card except Farmer John. He is a little upset…

It was Wednesday evening on Thistledown Farm and Farmer John was talking to Wendy his wife.

'Do you love me, Wendy?' he asked.

Wendy laughed. 'That's a strange question for a husband to ask his wife,' she said. 'Don't I cook and clean and look after the children and do the books and feed the calves for you?'

'Yes,' said Farmer John, 'but do you really love me?'

'I don't know,' said Wendy. 'Ask me later when I haven't got so much to do!'

Farmer John sat and watched the telly. There was a picture of a man holding a huge bunch of flowers in the shape of a red heart.

'Don't forget,' said the announcer, 'it's Saint Valentine's Day tomorrow, remember to send your loved ones a card.'

Farmer John sat up. 'What a good idea,' he said, and ran upstairs. He found a big piece of card and borrowed some coloured pens and some glue and glitter from Johnny and Jemima, his twins. He took everything into his bedroom and closed the door.

When he came out a while later he was looking very pleased with himself.

'What have you been doing, John?' asked Wendy as he came downstairs.

'Oh nothing,' said Farmer John casually.

'Hmm,' said Wendy, 'I think you're up to something, I can tell.'

'It's a secret,' said Farmer John. 'You'll find out soon enough.'

When they went to bed later that night Farmer John asked Wendy if she loved him again but Wendy just turned over and pretended she was asleep.

'Oh dear,' thought Farmer John. 'I hope she really does love me.' And he reached over and turned off the light.

When he woke up sunlight was streaming through the curtains. He yawned and stretched, then Wendy came in with a cup of tea. She was carrying a large red envelope.

'I wonder what this could be,' she said. 'It's got my name on it.'

Farmer John smiled. 'If it's got your name on it, it must be for you,' he said. 'Why don't you open it?'

Wendy tore open the envelope and pulled out a big glittery card with a huge red heart on it.

'Bless me,' she said. 'It's a valentine. I wonder who it's from.' She opened it up. Inside was a little poem.

Roses are red
Violets are blue
Sugar is sweet
And so are you!
Love from
Guess Who? XXX

'Goodness,' said Wendy. 'Someone must really love me! I wonder who on earth it could be?'

'Yes,' said Farmer John. 'I wonder.'

They dressed and went downstairs for breakfast but when Farmer John went to the mat to look for the morning post there weren't any cards for him.

'Haven't I got any cards at all?' said Farmer John.

'It doesn't look like it,' said Wendy.

'Oh dear,' thought Farmer John. 'Nobody loves me.' He began to feel a little sad.

He munched his breakfast in silence.

'Nobody cares about me,' he muttered to himself. 'I'm just here to work and work, everyone takes me for granted.' And he let out a little sigh.

'What was that dear?' asked Wendy from the kitchen.

'Oh nothing,' said Farmer John, and he went outside to feed his animals.

'Morning John,' mooed Daisy. The cows were standing in the yard after milking. 'Look what I got this morning.' Daisy produced a big card with lots of glittery pink hearts on it. 'It's a valentine,' she said. 'Go on, read what it says.'

Farmer John read the poem inside the card.

Roses are red
Violets are blue
Cows are black and white
And Nuns are too!
Love from
Guess Who? XXX

'That's nice,' said Farmer John. 'Do you know who sent it?'

'Well,' said Daisy, 'the handwriting looks familiar but I couldn't be sure.'

'You must have a secret admirer,' said Farmer John knowingly.

Farmer John went down to the pig-pens with a bag of sow nuts. He poured the sow nuts into the trough and the pigs came running out.

'WHEE!' said Suzie the sow. 'Look what I got this morning, John.'

Farmer John took the card from Suzie's trotter.

'It's another valentine,' he said. 'Someone certainly seems to be fond of my animals.' And he read the message inside the card.

> *Roses are red*
> *Violets are blue*
> *Piglets are pink*
> *And sows are too!*
> *Love from*
> *Guess Who? XXX*

'Do you know who it's from?' asked Farmer John.

'I'm not sure,' said Suzie. 'It could be anyone.'

'That's true,' said Farmer John rather sadly.

He finished with the pigs and went up to the sheep shed. Mavis the ewe was nibbling away on some hay.

'Baa,' she said. 'You look a bit fed up, John. What's the matter?'

'Nobody's sent me a valentine today,' said Farmer John.

'Oh,' said Mavis. 'I guess nobody loves you then.'

'But surely you don't need a valentine's card to be loved?' he said.

'Perhaps you're right,' said Mavis, 'but it's nice to get one, isn't it? Look.' And she showed Farmer John a glittery red card.

'You mean you got one too?' said Farmer John with a twinkle in his eye.

'Yes,' said Mavis. 'Do you want to see what it says?' Farmer John read:

> *Roses are red*
> *Violets are blue*
> *Sheep are cuddly*
> *And so are you!*
> *Love from*
> *Guess Who? XXX*

'I wonder who that could be from?' said Farmer John.

'I think I may have an idea,' said Mavis mysteriously.

Farmer John smiled. 'Well, Wendy and all my animals have got cards so everyone has one except me. Never mind, perhaps I'll get one next year.' He walked down across the yard to the farmhouse, but just as he got to the door Pete the postman drove up in his bright red van.

'Hello, John,' he said. 'I've got something for you', and he handed Farmer John a big box.

'Thank you, Pete,' said Farmer John. 'What could this be, I wonder?' He unwrapped the parcel. Inside was a large heart-shaped cake with the words *To John from all the animals and Wendy.*

Farmer John was overcome. 'Thank you very much, all of you,' he said as he wiped a tear from his eye. 'I thought that nobody cared.'

Wendy smiled. 'Perhaps you know the answer to your question now,' she said. 'Yes, I do really love you, you're the best husband in the county.'

Farmer John gave her a huge hug.

Everyone had a slice of his valentine's cake and they were all very happy because everybody loved each other very much on Thistledown Farm!

FARMER JOHN'S MUCKY DAY

Farmer John is mucking out his cow barn but Myrtle his muck-spreader has other ideas…

One bright morning Farmer John jumped out of bed and pulled the curtains. 'What a beautiful morning,' he said to Wendy his wife, 'just right to do some muck-spreading!'

Wendy laughed. 'Muck-spreading?' 'You're *always* muck-spreading, can't you find something less smelly to do?'

'But I like muck-spreading,' said Farmer John. 'I have to clean out my animals and the muck's good for the fields, it makes the grass grow!'

'Well,' said Wendy, 'if you must, but don't come anywhere near the house – I'm doing some washing today I don't want my clothes smelling of manure!'

They dressed and went downstairs for breakfast. Wendy piled Farmer John's plate with sausages, bacon, eggs, tomatoes, fried bread, beans and mushrooms.

'There you are,' she said. 'Hard-working farmers need feeding just like their animals!' Farmer John tucked into his breakfast. When he had finished he put on his boots and cap and went out into the yard.

He marched up to the tractor shed. Tommy the tractor was standing by the diesel tank. 'Come on, Tommy,' said Farmer John, 'we're going muck-spreading!'

'Yippee,' said Tommy, 'I love muck-spreading!'

Farmer John filled Tommy's tank with diesel and drove down the yard to find his muck-spreader.

Myrtle the muck-spreader was hiding. She was feeling a bit tired. She had just started to go back to sleep when Farmer John found her.

'Come on Myrtle,' he said, 'we've got lots to do today, rise and shine!'

Myrtle groaned. 'Can't you do something else?' she said. 'I'm feeling a bit sleepy this morning.'

'But you haven't done anything for ages,' said Farmer John.

'I know, but my chains and sprockets are stiff,' groaned Myrtle.

But Farmer John soon put that right. He found an oil-can and grease-gun and soon got Myrtle's chains and sprockets working nicely.

He drove up to the cow barn. The floor was covered in a thick black layer of rich manure. Farmer John had parked Linford the loader outside. He jumped into Linford's cab and pushed Lindford's fork into the dung, his wheels spinning. He lifted up a big chunk of muck and dumped it in Myrtle's barrel.

'OOF!' said Myrtle. 'Can't you be more careful? I'm feeling a bit sensitive this morning.'

Farmer John filled Myrtle's barrel with dung and drove off up the lane to the fields to go spreading. He pulled a lever in Tommy's cab and CLAC-CLAC-CLAC! – Myrtle's flails started to go round. WHOOSH! – a shower of muck flew out of her side onto the grass. Farmer John felt very happy. He began to sing a little song by 'The Wurzles'. 'Aye o liddle-iddle o, Chesterfield to Cheddar, aye o the folks all know I'm the champion dung-spreader!'

Myrtle wasn't quite so happy. 'I could do with a rest,' she thought, then she saw the flock of sheep in the next door field. They were having their mid-morning nap.

'Look at those lazy animals,' thought Myrtle. 'I wish I could sleep all day. I'll show them!' And she let out a huge splurge of muck. It went sailing over the hedge and landed SPLAT! all over Mavis the ewe.

'BAAH!' cried Mavis and jumped to her feet. She was covered from head to foot in smelly dung and had changed colour from white to black!

'HA HA!' laughed Myrtle. 'That'll teach you to sleep so close to me while I'm spreading dung.'

Mavis was very upset with Farmer John. 'Baa,' she bleated, 'blooming farmer, he ought to be more careful!'

Myrtle was enjoying herself. 'What can I do now,' she thought, then she saw the cows standing by the gate.

CLAC-CLAC-CLAC! Myrtle threw out a great wodge of black sticky dung SPLAT! all over Daisy the dairy cow.

'MOO!' cried Daisy. 'Look at me, I'm covered in POO!'

Myrtle laughed. 'HA HA! Stupid cows, don't they like getting mucky?'

'MOO,' Daisy went. 'Blooming farmer, he needs to watch what he's doooing!' Daisy was very cross with Farmer John.

But Farmer John didn't know, he was too busy singing his little song to notice anything wrong.

The pigs were snoring in the pig-pens when Myrtle went by. CLAC-CLAC-CLAC! A huge pile of manure sailed over the wall and landed PLOP! all over Suzie the sow.

'YEUK!' yelled Suzie. 'How disgusting! What *does* Farmer John think he's playing at?'

Meanwhile, Wendy was putting out her washing on the line. 'It's a nice day,' she thought, 'these won't take long to dry.'

Myrtle trundled by on her way to the field.

'HA!' she said. 'This is too good to miss.'

CLAC-CLAC-CLAC! A splurge of muck flew out of her side SPLAT! all over Wendy and her white sheets.

Wendy was very cross. 'Now I'll have to wash these all over again!' she fumed.

Mrs Jollyhocks was riding her horse Cyril TRIT-TROT along the bridlepath when there was a CLAC-CLAC-CLAC! A ginormous dollop of dung flew over the hedge and landed SQUELCH! all over her.

'Oh no!' she cried. 'I'm *covered* in dung!'

'Pooh,' said Cyril, 'you stink!'

When Farmer John got back to the yard he was confronted by Daisy, Suzie and Mavis. They were looking very cross and so were Mrs Jollyhocks and Wendy.

'JOHN STUBBLEFIELD!' they cried. 'You mucky man, look what you've done to us all!'

Farmer John laughed. 'Oh dear,' he said, 'did I do that? I'll have to be a bit more careful in future.'

Myrtle couldn't stop herself from laughing. She began to giggle and giggle and laugh and laugh. CLAC-CLAC-CLAC! Her flails went round and with a WHOOSH! a shower of muck flew out of her side SPLAT! all over Farmer John!

'YEUK!' said Farmer John. 'So it was you all along! You're a naughty, *naughty* muck-spreader, just because you like being mucky doesn't mean everyone else does. I think you deserve a bath!'

'Oh no,' said Myrtle, 'anything but a bath, I hate being clean!'

'Tough,' said Farmer John. 'It serves you right. Come on, everyone, let's take her to the river!'

So everyone took Myrtle down to the river and she fell in. They all jumped in to wash themselves off and everyone gave Myrtle a good scrubbing. She wasn't very happy at all, she didn't like soap!

'I hope that teaches you a lesson,' said Farmer John.

'Yes,' said Myrtle, 'I promise to be good as long as you promise never to give me a wash again.'

Farmer John laughed. 'OK,' he said, 'it's a deal.'

So from then on Myrtle behaved herself very well because although she had enjoyed making everyone else mucky, she certainly didn't want to be clean herself!

FARMER JOHN'S GOLDEN JUBILEE

The Queen is celebrating fifty years on the throne. Farmer John and Wendy are celebrating fifty years of farming!

It was breakfast time on Thistledown Farm and Farmer John was reading his newspaper. 'It says here,' he said to Wendy his wife, 'that the Queen has been on the throne for fifty years.'

'Goodness,' said Wendy, 'that's a long time to be sitting down!'

'Don't be silly, dear,' said Farmer John, 'how could anyone sit down for that long? It just means that the Queen has reigned for fifty years.'

'What! Rained for fifty years? What terrible weather,' said Wendy. 'I hope she has an umbrella!'

Farmer John sighed. 'Do you take *anything* I say seriously?' he said.

'No,' said Wendy. 'Hurry up and eat your breakfast, I've got to get to work.'

Farmer John gobbled down his bacon and eggs. He finished and pushed his plate away.

'As I was saying,' he continued, 'the Queen has been Queen for fifty years. It's her Golden Jubilee – are we going to do anything to celebrate?'

'I don't know,' said Wendy. 'Perhaps we could have a party.'

'That's a good idea,' said Farmer John. 'I'll think about it.' And he put on his cap and went out to feed his animals.

Wendy stood at the sink and washed up Farmer John's plate. 'Fifty years,' she thought. 'Hmm. I wonder…' She dried her hands and went to find her diary. She looked back through the pages. 'Here we are,' she said. 'Nineteen fifty-two, that's when Grand-dad started farming. Our family have been working here on Thistledown Farm for fifty years. Fifty years! It must be our Golden Jubilee too, we must have a celebration. A double Golden Jubilee – we need to do something special!'

She untied her apron and dashed out of the house to go to work.

When Farmer John came in that evening, Wendy was cooking dinner.

'I've been thinking about that Jubilee party,' he said. 'I think we should have a quiet little do, not too much fuss, just me and you and a few of the animals. We don't want to overdo it.'

'But John,' said Wendy, 'do you know what? It's our Jubilee too, we've been farming here for fifty years.'

'Really?' said Farmer John. 'It seems more like a hundred!'

'Why?' asked Wendy.

'Oh, I'm just tired,' said Farmer John, 'I've had a bad day. My sheep have got out, I've got a cow with a lame foot, Tommy my tractor has broken down and the birds are eating my crops!'

'Oh dear,' said Wendy, 'that's not very good.'

'Never mind,' said Farmer John. 'It's not all that bad. I had some lovely lambs born this morning and my cows are giving heaps of milk.'

'Thank goodness for that,' said Wendy. 'Why don't you put your feet up, dinner's nearly ready.'

Farmer John sat and watched the telly. It was the news. There was a picture of the Queen doing a Royal Tour. Thousands of people were cheering and waving flags. Farmer John sat up. 'Isn't she wonderful?' he said to Wendy. 'I don't know how she does it. I don't think I could smile and be nice to everyone all the time like that.'

'She's had lots of practice,' said Wendy, 'but she does it well, doesn't she? Aren't we lucky to have her as our Queen.'

Farmer John nodded. 'Perhaps we should have a bigger party,' he said, 'seeing as it's our Golden Jubilee too.'

So next day Wendy started making arrangements. She made a long, long list of everything she had to do. There was lots to think of. They had to hire a tent, book a band and some entertainers, decide what they wanted to eat and drink and she got quite excited.

Soon everything was ready and Farmer John and Wendy sent out invitations to all their friends and neighbours. Farmer John put up a huge marquee in the big field and bought lots and lots of fireworks. He was very excited and so were his animals, and when the big day came they were ready for a party.

Everyone filled the huge marquee. The band started to play and they all got up to dance. The pigs danced with the cows, the cows danced with the sheep and the sheep danced with the pigs. They did the foxtrot and the two-step and the waltz. They did the rhumba, the tango and the cha-cha-cha and they did the boogie, the twist and the jive.

When they got tired there was heaps to eat and drink. There was jelly and ice cream, sandwiches and sausage rolls, cake and sherry trifle and smoked salmon and champagne.

There were lots of entertainers. There was a man telling jokes, a belly dancer, a juggler, a magician and a fire-eater! Everyone had a whale of a time and they danced until they dropped. Finally they all trooped outside to watch the fireworks.

There were rockets and bangers and Catherine wheels. There were red ones and white ones and blue ones and ones that were soggy and refused to light. Everyone went 'OOH!' and 'AAH!' as they lit up the night sky.

When it was all over, everyone said how they couldn't remember when they'd last had such a good time and they all went to bed very happy.

Farmer John woke up the next morning with a bit of a sore head and Wendy brought them both a strong cup of coffee.

'There's a letter for you here,' she said, 'do you want to read it?'

'You open it,' said Farmer John, 'my eyes are a bit blurry this morning.'

Wendy opened the envelope and read the letter. 'JOHN!' she cried. 'It's from Buckingham Palace. You've been invited to be knighted!'

'What do you mean, invited to be knighted?' said Farmer John.

'It says you're going to be made a Sir for services to farming,' said Wendy. 'The Queen has heard that we've been farming for fifty years – isn't it marvellous!'

Farmer John sat up. 'Really?' he said, '*me*, a knight? Do I have to get a horse and a suit of armour?'

'Of course not,' laughed Wendy. 'You'll need a suit, though, if you're going to meet the Queen. I'd better go and look it out, it's ages since you wore it last.'

Farmer John scrambled out of bed. He looked at himself in the mirror.

'Sir John Stubblefield,' he said, 'I like the sound of that.'

'Don't go getting all big-headed, John,' said Wendy. 'You're still just a farmer, remember.'

It wasn't long before the day came when Farmer John had to go up to Buckingham Palace, but when Wendy found his suit it was full of moth holes.

'Oh my goodness, John,' she cried, 'you've got nothing to wear!'

'I'll go in my wellies,' said Farmer John. 'I'm sure the Queen won't mind.'

'You can't do that,' said Wendy, 'what *will* people think of you?'

'I don't care,' said Farmer John, 'I'll wear my best pair!'

He got out his poshest wellies and polished them and polished them and polished them until they shone so much that he could see his face in them. He brushed all the straw off his cap and put it on his head.

'There,' he said, 'I'm ready.'

When Farmer John and Wendy arrived at Buckingham Palace, he got some funny looks from the footman at the door.

'And who are *you*?' said the footman.

'I'm John Stubblefield,' said Farmer John. 'I've come to be knighted.'

The footman looked at his list. 'Ah yes, sir, follow me.'

Farmer John followed the footman into Buckingham Palace. He felt a little small in such grand surroundings, there were lots of huge paintings on the walls.

The footman opened a door. 'John Stubblefield, Ma'am,' he said, and ushered Farmer John inside.

The Queen was standing in the middle of the room. Farmer John took off his cap. He walked towards a cushion and knelt down. The Queen took a long sword and Farmer John thought she was going to cut off his head but she just touched his shoulders with the blade.

'Arise, Sir John Stubblefield,' she said.

Farmer John got up. The Queen looked at Farmer John's wellies. Then she smiled. 'Do you *like* farming?' she asked.

'Oh yes,' said Farmer John, 'it's my life, I'd never do anything else.'

'How perfectly splendid,' said the Queen. She pinned a medal on Farmer John's shirt. 'Fifty years of farming is quite an achievement,' she said.

'Yes,' said Farmer John, 'and so is fifty years on the throne.'

The Queen offered him her hand. Farmer John kissed it. 'If you're ever down our way,' said Farmer John, 'you'd be very welcome to visit Thistledown Farm.'

'I'd be delighted,' said the Queen. 'I've heard so much about it.'

At the reception afterwards, Farmer John had a little bit too much champagne and on the way home he started singing songs on the underground. Wendy had to shut him up!

When he got back he showed everyone his medal. They were very impressed.

'Do we have to call you Sir John now?' asked his animals.

'I don't think so,' said Farmer John. 'I may have met the Queen but I'm only a simple farmer really so just plain John will be fine enough for me.'

Wendy gave him a huge hug. 'You're my knight in shining armour,' she said.

Farmer John smiled. 'More like shining wellies,' he said and he toddled off to do some farming.

FARMER JOHN'S ROYAL VISIT

The Queen comes to visit Thistledown Farm but Farmer John soon ropes her into doing some farm work!

One bright morning Farmer John woke up and stretched. He yawned and opened his eyes. 'What a lovely morning,' he said to Wendy his wife, 'what's happening today, dear?'

'I don't know,' said Wendy, 'but I expect something will, something's always happening on Thistledown Farm.'

Farmer John smiled. 'Yes,' he said, 'life on Thistledown Farm is never dull.'

They dressed and went downstairs for breakfast.

'I think I'll do some odd jobs today, dear,' said Farmer John. 'I've got fences to mend and some pig-pens to muck out. It's a nice day, I think I'll get on with that.'

'Good idea,' said Wendy, and she gave him a plate of sausages, bacon and eggs.

Farmer John munched his sausages. Just then the phone rang.

'Can you go?' said Wendy. 'I'm in the middle of something.'

Farmer John jumped up with a mouthful of sausage. He picked up the receiver.

'Good morning,' said a voice. 'Can I speak to Sir John Stubblefield please?'

'Speaking,' mumbled Farmer John through his sausages.

'This is Buckingham Palace,' said the voice. 'The Queen has heard so much about Thistledown Farm that she wishes to visit you today. She will be coming at nine o'clock this morning.'

Farmer John gulped. 'This morning!' he cried, 'Nine o'clock? But it's already eight-thirty!'

'Is that a problem?' said the voice.

'No, no, of course not,' said Farmer John hastily, 'it will be an honour!' He put down the receiver and dashed into the kitchen. 'WENDY!' he cried. 'The Queen is coming in half an hour, what are we going to do?'

'Heavens,' said Wendy, 'the place is a mess! We'd better get tidied up.' She rushed to find her vacuum cleaner.

Farmer John went out into the yard. He stared around him. There were piles of rusty old tin, coils of rusty barbed wire, old fertilizer sacks were scattered everywhere and lots of old car tyres were lying around. Next to the workshop were some broken old gates and by the woodshed was a pile of rotting logs!

'Oh dear,' thought Farmer John. 'What am I going to do with all this junk? I know, I'll chuck it all in a big heap behind the barn. The Queen will never see it there.'

He got a wheelbarrow and started moving all the rubbish. It took him many trips and when he had finished he was quite exhausted.

'There,' he said, 'that's that done, now I'd better clean the yard, the Queen doesn't want to see a mucky farmyard.'

He found a shovel and a brush and began brushing the yard down. He brushed and he brushed and he brushed until his back ached. Finally he straightened up. 'That's better,' he said. He was quite out of breath when a huge black shiny car with a flag flying from the roof rolled into the yard. A chauffeur got out and opened the door. The Queen stepped out.

'Your Majesty,' puffed Farmer John. 'Welcome to Thistledown Farm!'

'Enchanted,' said the Queen. She looked around the farmyard. 'What a tidy farm,' she said smiling. 'It's so nice to see a well-kept farmyard.'

Farmer John grinned. 'Thank you, Your Majesty,' he said. 'I like to keep things tidy! Do you have any gumboots, Ma'am?' he asked.

'I was hoping I might borrow a pair,' said the Queen. 'Mine have a hole in.'

'Of course,' said Farmer John. 'Wait there.' And he nipped into the farmhouse and brought out a pair of his poshest wellies. 'They might be a bit big,' he said.

'That's all right,' said the Queen, 'I've got thick socks on.'

'I'm afraid I haven't milked the cows yet,' said Farmer John. 'Would you like to help?'

'Oh yes,' said the Queen, 'I love cows.'

'We'll have to go and fetch them,' said Farmer John, 'it's a bit of a walk but you'll be able to see the farm then.'

'How nice,' said the Queen, and she followed Farmer John through the yard and across the fields to get the cows. He pointed out all the fields on the way.

'That's the big field,' he said, 'where we had our Golden Jubilee party and that's my favourite tree, and over there is the river where Myrtle my muck-spreader fell in once.'

'Goodness!' said the Queen. 'Was she all right?'

'Oh yes,' said Farmer John. 'She was being a bit naughty, I'm afraid, she was covering everybody with dung but she's learnt her lesson. She's behaving herself very well now.'

'I'm glad to hear it,' said the Queen.

They brought the cows in from the fields and started milking. Daisy was very surprised when she realised who was milking her. 'Moo!' she said. 'Your Majesty, what an honour!'

'May I present Your Majesty with Daisy,' said Farmer John. 'She's my best milker. She always wins first prize at the county show every year.'

'I'm delighted to meet you, Daisy,' said the Queen.

Daisy blushed.

When they had finished milking the cows Farmer John asked the Queen if she wouldn't mind helping him with a few little jobs.

'Of course,' said the Queen, 'I'd love to help.'

So Farmer John took the Queen to his workshop. They collected a hammer and some nails, a saw and some timber and put them in a trailer. Farmer John jumped up into his tractor cab and the Queen perched next to him. They drove off up the lane to a place where there was a gap in the hedge. Farmer John jumped out and started building a fence. The Queen gave him a hand. Farmer John held a wooden stake and the Queen knocked it into the ground with a big hammer.

'There,' said Farmer John, 'that's one done, only ten more to do!'

The Queen got a bit warm with knocking fence posts in, it was quite hard work! When they had finished they sat down and ate some sandwiches.

'How lovely to be sitting in the countryside eating sandwiches,' said the Queen. 'All that hard work has made me feel quite hungry.'

But they weren't able to sit down for long. Farmer John's sheep had got out. They weren't in the field where they belonged.

'Would Your Majesty mind helping me with my sheep?' asked Farmer John.

'Of course not,' said the Queen. 'I'd be delighted.'

The Queen and Farmer John began chasing his sheep around the field. They were very silly and didn't want to go through an open gateway. The Queen got very hot and bothered with chasing them around.

Eventually, though, the sheep went back where they belonged.

'Goodness,' puffed the Queen, 'that was good exercise! Running around after sheep must keep you very fit.'

'Yes,' said Farmer John, 'it does!'

Farmer John let the Queen get her breath back.

'Now if you don't mind,' he said, 'I've got another little job you could help me with.'

'Oh,' said the Queen, 'do I have to?'

'It won't take very long,' said Farmer John. 'I need you to help muck out my pigs!'

'If I must,' said the Queen, 'but then I think I really must be going. I have some important matters to attend to. I have to open Parliament.'

'That can wait,' said Farmer John. 'My pigs are far more important!'

He gave the Queen a fork and a wheelbarrow. 'Here are the pigs, Ma'am,' he said. 'Now, I'll just leave you to get on with it while I go and have a cup of tea.' He pushed off, leaving the Queen forking manure!

'Is the Queen all right?' asked Wendy, when he came in.

'Oh yes,' said Farmer John. 'She's doing very well. She's helped me with the milking, built a fence, chased some sheep around and now I've got her cleaning out my pigs.'

'WHAT!' cried Wendy. 'You can't be serious!'

'She's being very helpful,' said Farmer John. 'She doesn't seem to mind.'

'JOHN STUBBLEFIELD, you *stupid* man! You mean to tell me that the Queen kindly came to pay you a visit and you made her muck out your pigs! I don't believe it. Sometimes I think you've got no sense at all. What *are* you thinking of?'

Farmer John was a little taken aback. 'But Wendy,' he cried, 'I was going to pay her.'

'PAY HER!' said Wendy. 'But the Queen doesn't need your money, she's got plenty enough of her own. I think you need your head looking at!'

'Rubbish,' said Farmer John. 'She's enjoying it, a bit of hard work never hurt anyone. Besides, she's got nothing else to do, only open Parliament.'

'Well,' said Wendy, 'that's OK then, but I think you'd better go and see how she's getting on. We don't want to tire her out.'

But just then the Queen came to the door. 'I've finished,' she said. 'Can I go now?'

'Of course,' said Farmer John, 'but before you do let me give you this.' He got out his wallet and took out a used five-pound note. 'There,' he said, 'I think you've earned it!'

The Queen took the money. 'Thank you,' she said, 'that will come in very handy.'

'Don't forget to give me back my gumboots,' said Farmer John.

'Can I keep them as a memento?' said the Queen.

'Of course,' said Farmer John, 'by all means.'

'I'll think of you whenever I wear them,' said the Queen. 'I've had such an interesting day!'

'I'm glad,' said Farmer John. 'Would you like to come and visit us again?'

'I don't know,' said the Queen. 'It's been quite an experience but I think I'm going to be *very* busy for quite some time!'

And she got into her car and disappeared off up the lane.

FARMER JOHN'S MARCH

The Council plans to demolish Thistledown Farm. Farmer John holds a protest...

One fine morning Farmer John jumped out of bed and pulled the curtains.

'What a lovely day,' he said to Wendy his wife, 'what could possibly go wrong on a day like this?'

Wendy laughed. 'Oh I expect something will,' she said, 'you're always getting into trouble.'

'Rubbish,' said Farmer John. 'I'm the best farmer in the county, nothing ever goes wrong on Thistledown Farm.'

They dressed and went downstairs for breakfast. Wendy piled Farmer John's plate with sausages, bacon, eggs, tomatoes, fried bread, beans and mushrooms.

'There you are,' she said. 'Hard-working farmers need feeding just like their animals!'

Farmer John tucked into his breakfast. When he had finished he put on his boots and cap and went out into the yard. He was just about to go up to the sheep shed when a smart red car pulled up outside. A man got out. He was wearing a shiny new suit and a shiny new pair of shoes. He was wearing a bowler hat and carried a rolled up umbrella.

'Excuse me,' said the man, 'is this Thistledown Farm?'

Farmer John nodded.

'Well,' continued the man, 'I won't beat about the bush. I'm from the Council. This farm is to be demolished. We're going to build a new town on this land, we need lots more houses, I'm afraid you'll have to go!'

'WHAT!' cried Farmer John. 'You can't build houses on Thistledown Farm. You must be joking.'

'It's no joke,' said the man and he got out a map and put it on the bonnet of his car. 'These are the plans,' he said. Farmer John looked over the man's shoulder. 'Here is Thistledown Farm,' said the man, 'and here is where the new town is to be. They're in the same place. You'll have to start looking for somewhere else to live.'

'But what will happen to all my animals?' said Farmer John.

'I don't know,' said the man, 'that's not my problem.'

Farmer John gave the man a hard stare. 'Now look here,' he said. 'I don't know who you think you are but I'm not going anywhere. You'll just have to find somewhere else to put your new town.'

The man laughed. 'My dear fellow,' he said. 'It's all been decided. Once the Council has made up its mind, there's no changing it, I'm afraid.'

'But isn't there anything I can do!' cried Farmer John.

'No,' said the man, 'your situation is hopeless. I'm sorry but you might as well start packing now.'

He got back into his car and drove off without a toot.

Farmer John started to panic. He rushed into the farmhouse.

'WENDY!' he cried. 'You'll never guess what! They're going to build a new town on Thistledown Farm, we're going to have to leave.'

'WHAT!' said Wendy. 'A new town, are you sure?'

'YES,' said Farmer John, flapping his arms. 'A man in a bowler hat just came, he said we might as well start packing now!'

Wendy looked a bit shocked.

'But surely they've got enough towns without building any more?' she said.

'That's what I thought,' said Farmer John, 'but the Council has made up its mind and there's nothing we can do about it.'

'Hmm,' said Wendy. 'Is that so? We'll have to see about this.' And she went into the kitchen and closed the door. She came out a little while later with a smile on her face.

'I've had an idea,' she said.

Farmer John jumped up. 'Really?' he said. 'Have you got a plan?'

'Yes,' said Wendy, 'we're going to hold a protest.'

'A protest!' said Farmer John. 'What sort of a protest?'

'We're going to march on the town hall,' said Wendy. 'The Council will have to take notice of us if we do that.'

'What a good idea,' said Farmer John. 'I'll have to tell the animals.' And he rushed out of the house.

Mavis the ewe was nibbling some hay when Farmer John arrived.

'Baa,' said Mavis. 'Morning, John, what's happening today?'

'I'll tell you what's happening,' said Farmer John. 'The Council are planning to build houses on Thistledown Farm and we're going to hold a protest. Do you want to join in?'

'Baa,' said Mavis, 'of course. It sounds exciting.'

'Good,' said Farmer John. 'I knew you would. You'd better get all the sheep together, it's going to be a very big thing.'

He left Mavis and ran over to the cow yard. Daisy was standing by the water trough.

'Moo,' she said. 'Morning, John, what's up with you? You look a bit wild!'

'I am,' said Farmer John. 'The Council are going to build a new town on Thistledown Farm. We're going to do something to stop them, will you join us?'

'Oh yes,' said Daisy. 'What are we going to dooo?'

'We're marching on the town hall,' said Farmer John. 'You'd better get all the cows ready, we're going as soon as we can.'

Farmer John hurried down to the pig-pens. Suzie the sow was scratching herself on the pig-pen wall.

'Morning, Suzie,' said Farmer John. 'You'd better get all the pigs together. We're going on a protest march.'

'WHEE,' said Suzie, 'how exciting!'

'If we don't protest,' said Farmer John, 'we'll all lose our homes and we won't have anywhere to live.'

'OINK,' said Suzie. Don't worry, John, I'm a pig, I'm good at protesting!'

Wendy was making some banners when Farmer John got back to the farmhouse. She had torn up some sheets and painted words all over them. Farmer John read the banners. *SAVE THISTLEDOWN FARM* he read, and *DOWN WITH THE COUNCIL.*

'What about *NO NEW HOUSES*?' he said.

'Good idea,' said Wendy, 'and we'll need some for the animals.'

'What about *THE PIGS ARE REVOLTING*?' said Farmer John.

Wendy laughed. 'OK, and how about the cows?'

'*COWS AGAINST THE COUNCIL*,' said Farmer John, 'and *SAVE OUR SHEEP.*'

Wendy got busy with the paint pot.

Farmer John hitched up Tommy the tractor to Myrtle the muck-spreader.

'Come on, Myrtle' he said, 'let's show that Council what we're made of.'

Wendy and all the animals followed him down the road. Farmer John drove very slowly and all the animals chanted and waved their banners, and the cows sang 'WE SHALL NOT BE MOOOVED!' Everyone on the way waved and clapped and honked their horns as they went by.

When they reached Dexeter they held up the traffic and everyone looked very cross. Finally they got to the town hall. They stood outside and chanted 'NO NEW HOUSES' and blew whistles. The man in the bowler hat came out onto the steps and tried to talk to them but he couldn't hear himself speak with all the noise. He stepped down and came to argue with Farmer John, Farmer John ignored him but the man began to poke him with his finger! Farmer John decided he'd had enough.

'Come on, Myrtle!' he cried. 'Show them what we think of them!'

CLAC-CLAC-CLAC! Myrtle's flails started to go round and with a WHOOSH! a shower of muck flew out of her side SPLAT! all over the man in the bowler hat.

'GRRR!' said the man. 'YEUK, look at me, I'm covered in dung!'

Farmer John laughed. 'That's what we think of your plans,' he said.

The man in the bowler hat looked very cross. 'I'm going to call the police!' he said.

It wasn't long before PC Collar turned up in his smart police car. He squeezed himself out.

'What seems to be the problem?' he said. Then he saw the man in the bowler hat. 'Oh dear,' he said to Farmer John. 'What *have* you been up to? I hope you're keeping within the law.'

'This is a peaceful protest,' said Farmer John. 'We're trying to save Thistledown Farm.'

The policeman looked around. The animals were chaining themselves to the railings. He laughed.

'Well,' he said, 'you certainly seem to be well organised. There's nothing much I can do, just make sure it doesn't get out of hand.'

'But aren't you going to arrest him?' screamed the man in the bowler hat.

The policeman laughed.

'Accidents *will* happen,' he said.

The man fumed.

Next day, when all the animals, Wendy and Farmer John had got back to Thistledown Farm, the protest was in all the newspapers and on TV. Farmer John, Wendy, Daisy, Suzie and Mavis sat round to watch.

'Well,' said Farmer John, 'it looks like we made an impression.'

'Yes,' said Wendy, 'I wonder if it will do any good?'

Just then there was a knock at the door. Wendy got up to open it. A man stood outside.

'Hello,' he said, 'I'm from the government. We heard about your protest and I've come to tell you that we're making Thistledown Farm an Area of Outstanding Natural Beauty. Thistledown Farm is so beautiful that it would be a crime to build houses on it. That Council will have to build elsewhere now, I thought you'd be glad to know.'

Everyone jumped to their feet.

'YES!' they all cried and danced around and hugged each other.

Wendy hugged the man. 'Oh thank you,' she said, 'we were all very worried.'

'Don't mention it,' said the man, 'it was the least we could do.'

That evening Farmer John held a huge party and everyone danced into the night and they were all very happy because they were so glad to have saved Thistledown Farm.

FARMER JOHN'S CIRCUS

Farmer John takes his family to see a circus. He decides to hold a circus of his own!

One day Farmer John was walking through town when he saw a big colourful poster on the wall. It said 'Billy Clark's Circus, Dexeter playing fields, Sunday March 13th, tickets £10'. Farmer John got very excited. 'I've never seen a circus before,' he said to himself. 'I must go. I'll take Wendy and the twins.'

When he got back to the farm Wendy his wife was in the kitchen.

'I've done your tea, John, hurry up and eat it before it gets cold.'

Farmer John smiled. 'What would I do without you, Wendy?' he said. 'It's not everyone who has their meals cooked for them.'

'Yes,' said Wendy,' but hard-working farmers need feeding just like their animals.'

Farmer John tucked into his steak and chips. 'I've been to town today,' he said, 'and guess what I saw?'
'How am I supposed to know?' said Wendy.
'I'll tell you then,' said Farmer John. 'I saw a poster for the Circus. It's coming on March 13th. Would you like to go? I would. We could take Johnny and Jemima.'

'What a good idea,' said Wendy. 'It's ages since I've been to see a circus.'

So that Sunday they all got dressed up smartly and drove off into town. There were lots of people there all crowding round a huge marquee with flags flying from the top. Music was coming from inside.

'We're just in time,' said Farmer John. 'Come on.' And they paid their money and took their seats inside the big top.

A man in a top hat carrying a whip came into the ring and announced to everyone that the show was about to begin.

'Ladies and gentlemen, let's have a big hand for Flip and Flop the acrobats.'

Two men in tights came into the ring and began to perform somersaults and cartwheels. They jumped and leapt all over the place and the crowd was soon clapping loudly.

'Gosh!' said Farmer John. 'I wish I was as bendy as them, it's as much as I can do to touch my toes. They must be made out of rubber!'

Johnny and Jemima were very impressed by the acrobats. 'I can do handstands and cartwheels,' said Jemima.

'I can do back-flips and forward rolls,' said Johnny.

'Perhaps you should join the circus,' said Farmer John. 'It must be an interesting life.'

'I don't know,' said Wendy, 'it looks a bit dangerous to me.'

'And now,' called the ringmaster, 'the high wire act.' A man stood by a ladder right at the top of the tent. He carried a long pole and started walking very slowly across a tightrope. Everyone held their breath as the drums rolled. He got to the middle and began to wobble. The crowd gasped.

'He's going to fall!' whispered Johnny.

'No he's not,' said Jemima. 'It's an act.'

He finally got across to the other end. The crowd sighed with relief.

'And now,' said the ringmaster, 'the trapeze!'

Two girls in tutus were swinging on bars up high, backwards and forwards, hanging by their knees. Then one of them grabbed hold of the other by the hands. The second girl let go of her trapeze and they swung back and forth together. Then one of them jumped back again and caught the empty bar. They made it look so easy.

'I'd love to be able to do that,' said Wendy.

'It makes me feel ill just looking,' said Farmer John. 'I used to get ill just sitting on a swing when I was a boy.'

'And now,' said the ringmaster, 'THE CLOWNS!'

A gang of clowns with painted faces and red noses came into the ring. They were carrying what looked like a bucket of water with them but when they threw it at the audience, it was only pieces of paper.

'Ho Ho Ho!' laughed Farmer John. 'They thought they were going to get soaked!'

The clowns played silly tricks, pushing each other over and putting things down each other's baggy trousers. They tripped over their long shoes and ended with a huge custard pie fight. The crowd roared; Johnny and Jemima couldn't stop laughing.

'I'd love to be a clown,' said Johnny.

'So would I,' said Farmer John.

The ringmaster came in to shoo the clowns out. 'And now, at last, the moment you've all been waiting for!' he boomed. 'THE HUMAN CANNONBALL!'

A huge gun appeared and a man wearing a cape and a crash helmet climbed inside. The drums rolled and with a bang and a flash he went sailing through the air and landed in a net. The crowd cheered.

When Farmer John and his family got outside it was dark and everyone was getting into their cars to go home. But when Wendy and the twins looked for him, Farmer John, it seemed, had suddenly disappeared.

'Where's he gone?' said Wendy crossly. 'It's past your bedtime, you two, you've got school in the morning.'

Farmer John came back with a funny smile on his face.

'What have you been up to?' said Wendy.

'I've had an idea,' said Farmer John. 'Just you wait and see.'

Next day a big lorry came into the farmyard with 'Billy Clark's Circus' written on it. 'Here's the Big Top that you asked for,' said the man to Farmer John. 'Just sign on the dotted line.'

Farmer John wasted no time in putting up the big marquee and all his animals got very excited. 'What's he going to do now?' they asked.

'I don't know,' mooed Daisy, 'he's always up to something crazy, that's why life on Thistledown Farm is never dull.'

'Right,' said Farmer John when he had gathered everyone together. 'We're going to be a circus and I want you all to do an act. Daisy, you can do the high wire, Suzie the trapeze and Mavis, you can be the sheep cannonball.'

'Baa,' said Mavis, 'not on your life!'

'It's easy,' said Farmer John, 'it doesn't hurt and it's quite safe. It'll be something to tell your lambs about.'

'Oh, OK, if you say so,' said Mavis, 'but what are you going to do?'

'I'm going to be a clown,' said Farmer John, 'and Wendy will be the ringmaster.'

Everyone practised their acts. Daisy walked the tightrope and soon got the hang of it. 'Moo,' she said. 'My mother always said I had a good head for heights.'

Suzie swung back and forth very merrily on the trapeze jumping from one to the other. 'WHEEE,' she sang, 'look at me, a flying pig!'

Johnny and Jemima practised tumbling acrobatics and Farmer John went around throwing custard pies at everybody. When they were all ready Farmer John advertised on the radio and hundreds of people turned up to watch the show.

Wendy came into the ring in a top hat and riding boots, carrying a whip. 'Welcome to John Stubblefield's Circus,' she announced. 'Bring on the acrobats!'

Johnny and Jemima came in doing cartwheels and handstands, back-flips and somersaults. The crowd cheered.

'And now for the high-wire act,' said Wendy. Daisy wobbled onto the tightrope.

The crowd gasped. 'Look mummy,' said a boy, 'it's a cow!'

'Yes,' said his mum. 'Farmer John's cows are very clever, you know.' Daisy made it across the rope and the crowd let out a sigh of relief. She made a bow. Everyone applauded.

Up above on the trapeze, Suzie the sow swung backwards and forwards. 'La, la la la la,' played the band and, to a loud drum roll, Suzie jumped across and caught the other trapeze. The crowd sang, 'She flies through the air with the greatest of ease, Farmer John's pig on her flying trapeze.' Everyone hooted with laughter.

Next, Farmer John came in with a big red nose. 'It's Dusty the clown,' announced Wendy. Farmer John ran in and tripped over, falling flat on his face. The crowd roared. He got up and fell down again. Then he pulled a string of sausages out of his trousers and everyone split their sides. He found a custard pie and gave it to Wendy to hold but she put it SPLAT! in his face. Poor Farmer John, everyone was laughing at him but he didn't mind, he was having fun.

A flock of sheep came in and began to climb up one on another until they made a big pyramid. 'Ta da!' the band went, and the sheep walked around the ring, balancing on one another's shoulders. The crowd whistled, then a herd of cows came in and walked around in a circle holding each other's tails in their mouths. Everyone cheered and clapped.

'And now,' said Wendy, '*the pièce de résistance*, MAVIS THE WOOLLY CANNONBALL!'

Mavis trotted into the ring with a crash helmet on. She hopped into the barrel of the gun and BANG! It went off. With a puff of smoke, Mavis shot through the air across the tent and landed BOING! in the net.

'BAA,' she went. 'That was fun, can I do it again?'

The crowd rose to their feet, cheering, whistling and clapping. They'd certainly had their money's worth.

After the performance a man came up to Farmer John. 'Hello,' he said. 'I'm the circus manager and I am so impressed by your acts I'm going to make you an offer you can't refuse.'

'Oh yes,' said Farmer John, 'what's that then?'

'I want your animals to come on tour with me,' he said. 'I'd pay well and it would be a new experience for them.'

Farmer John chuckled. 'What a good idea,' he said. 'Take them with you by all means.'

So all Farmer John's animals went off on tour with the circus and Farmer John took Wendy and his twins on holiday.

When his animals eventually came back, Farmer John held a welcome home party and everyone danced into the night because although they had all had a good time, they were glad to be back on Thistledown Farm again.

FARMER JOHN'S LONDON VISIT

Farmer John's sheep are bored. Farmer John takes them on a trip around London!

It was early in the morning on Thistledown Farm and Farmer John was talking to his sheep. 'You look a bit miserable this morning,' he said, 'what's the matter?'

Mavis the ewe nibbled some hay. 'Baa,' she said, 'we're so bored. We never go anywhere or do anything, it's so quiet on Thistledown Farm, we need some action!'

Farmer John laughed. 'Where do you want to go?' he asked.

Mavis pondered for a moment. 'Somewhere where there's lots going on,' she said. 'Somewhere where there's bright lights and music and things to do and see.'

'Goodness,' said Farmer John. 'It sounds like you want to go to London!'

'Baa,' went the sheep. 'LONDON! Yees, we want to go to London!'

Farmer John smiled. 'Well,' he said, 'it's a nice day, I haven't got much to do, why don't I take you!'

The sheep cheered and danced around. 'HOORAY!' they cried. 'WE'RE ALL OFF TO LONDON, WE'RE

ALL OFF TO LONDON, TA DA DA DA, TA DA DA DA!'

Farmer John roared with laughter. 'That's cheered you up,' he said. 'Now you'd better get ready. I'll be back to pick you up after breakfast.'

He marched back to the farmhouse. Wendy his wife was cooking bacon and eggs when he got in.

'Morning dear,' she said. 'How are the sheep?'

'Oh, they're very happy,' said Farmer John. 'I'm taking them to London today.'

'WHAT!' said Wendy. 'You can't be serious.'

'They're getting bored,' said Farmer John. 'I'm giving them a day out. It's a special treat.'

'But you can't take sheep to London,' said Wendy. 'What are you going to do with them?'

'I'm going to show them the sights,' said Farmer John. 'There's lots to do in London, they said they wanted some action and I'm going to give it to them!'

'Well,' said Wendy, 'I hope you know what you're doing!'

'Don't worry, my dear,' said Farmer John. 'I've been to London before, those sheep are going to have a great time, they'll really enjoy themselves.' He gobbled down his bacon and eggs, pulled on his cap and wellies and went out into the yard.

Lawrence the Landrover was waiting outside. He was very excited, he'd never been to London before.

'Come on, Lawrence,' said Farmer John. 'Let's get those sheep loaded up.' He hitched Lawrence up to a stock trailer and drove up to the sheep shed. 'Are you ready, girls?' he cried.

'Yeees,' bleated the sheep. 'We can't wait.'

The sheep piled into the trailer and Farmer John closed the door. 'All aboard,' he said, and drove off down the road.

It was quite a long journey and the sheep amused themselves by waving at car drivers on the motorway. They were quite surprised to be overtaken by a trailer load of waving sheep but they soon laughed and waved back.

Lawrence went as fast as he could and it wasn't too long before they reached London. Farmer John found a place to park in Trafalgar Square and the sheep jumped out onto the pavement. 'Baa,' they went, and stared around them. There were cars and buses, vans and taxis and lots and lots of hurrying people. Some of them stopped and stared with their mouths open.

They'd never seen a flock of sheep in London before!

Farmer John stopped the traffic and led the sheep across the road. There was a tall pillar with a statue of a man on the top. 'That's Nelson's Column,' said Farmer John. 'He was a great sea captain, and there are the lions!' The sheep were a bit afraid. 'Don't worry,' said Farmer John, 'they're only bronze lions.' The sheep were relieved.

'Now I expect you're a bit thirsty after your journey,' said Farmer John. 'There's a big fountain over there, go and have a drink in that.' So the sheep trotted over to the fountain and sipped some water. A flock of pigeons came down to talk to them.

'Coo,' they said, 'what are you?'

'We're sheep,' said the sheep. 'We come from the countryside.'

'OOH,' said the pigeons, 'we'd love to live in the countryside.'

'Baa,' said the sheep, 'it's boring, there's nothing to do so we've come up to London to see the sights.'

'Coo,' said the pigeons. 'Go and see Buckingham Palace, you must see Buckingham Palace.' And they all took off in a flurry and flap of wings and feathers.

'Come on,' said Farmer John. 'Don't waste time, what do you want to see first?'

'BUUUCKINGHAM PAALACE,' bleated the sheep.

So Farmer John led the sheep along the road. They went as fast as they could on their little legs but by the time they got to Buckingham Palace, there was a long queue of impatient car-, bus- and taxi-drivers hooting behind them! The drivers shouted angrily as they went past.

'Oh dear,' thought the sheep, 'everyone's in such a hurry.'

'Never mind them,' laughed Farmer John. 'People in London are always in a rush. Come on, here's the palace, let's go in and have a look.'

Farmer John paid the man at the door. 'How much do you charge for sheep?' he asked.

'Sheep go free,' said the man.

Farmer John led the sheep into Buckingham Palace. They all felt a little small in such grand surroundings. There were lots of huge paintings on the walls.

'Do you think we'll see the Queen?' asked the sheep.

'I'm afraid not,' said Farmer John. 'I think she's on holiday.'

The sheep were a bit disappointed. They began to nibble the curtains and carpets. Farmer John thought it was time to go! 'Come on,' he said, and he led the sheep out of Buckingham Palace and down the road to an underground station. 'We're going on a tube train,' he said.

The sheep followed him down some steps and down some more steps and onto an escalator. They were a bit scared of getting onto the moving staircase but Farmer John showed them how to do it. 'It's quite easy,' he said, 'once you've got the knack.'

People coming up the escalator on the other side were most surprised to see a farmer with a flock of sheep going down!

Once at the bottom, Farmer John and the sheep stood on the platform and when a train came rushing in, they all hopped on board. There wasn't much room and they all had to stand. Passengers sitting down were giving Farmer John some funny looks over their newspapers!

When they got to the other end, people coming down the escalator were very surprised to see Farmer John with a flock of sheep going up!

'Here we are,' said Farmer John. 'The London Eye.'

'What's the London Eye?' bleated the sheep.

'It's a big wheel,' said Farmer John. 'The biggest big wheel in the world.'

The sheep were very excited. 'Baa, can we go on it?' they pleaded. 'Please, John, please?'

Farmer John laughed. 'All right,' he said. He paid the man at the gate.

'I'm sorry, sir,' said the man, 'but sheep are not allowed.'

'But we're from Thistledown Farm!' cried Farmer John.

'Then why didn't you say so, sir!' said the man, and let them all in.

They got into a big glass capsule. It was a bit of a squeeze with all those sheep but Farmer John managed to get the doors shut. They started climbing very slowly up into the air.

Down below them all the cars, buses and taxis looked like tiny toys and the people scurrying along the pavements like busy ants. All the buildings were little boxes and the parks no more than small gardens. Some of the sheep felt a bit giddy with the height and had to shut their eyes! When they got to the very top they could all see for miles. The sheep were a bit disappointed that they couldn't see any fields.

Farmer John laughed. 'London's a very big place,' he said. 'There used to be fields a long time ago but they've all been built over now.'

When they got to the bottom again, the sheep followed Farmer John to a bus stop. A bright red double-decker bus came along and they all hopped aboard. They went upstairs. It was an open topped bus and Farmer John and his sheep sat at the front. They went through Piccadilly Circus, round Marble Arch, and down the Strand. They went along Oxford Street, past the Ritz Hotel and Buckingham Palace. They went by the Tower of London, across Tower Bridge over

the River Thames and past the Houses of Parliament and Big Ben and Westminster Abbey. They went through Camden Town, Notting Hill and Paddington, and passed St. Paul's Cathedral. The sheep had never seen so many places before and Farmer John was very pleased that they were enjoying themselves so much.

Finally the bus came to a stop. 'Here we are,' said Farmer John. 'Everybody off. It's Wimbledon, I don't think you've been to see a tennis match before.'

'Baa,' the sheep bleated. 'What's tennis?'

'It's a game,' said Farmer John. 'You hit a ball back and forward across a net with a racket.'

'Baa,' said the sheep, 'that doesn't sound too exciting.'

'Oh, but it is,' said Farmer John, 'you wait and see.'

They took their seats and two tennis players in shorts came out onto the tennis court. They bowed to the Royal Box and started to play. They were very good at it and they made each other work very hard. It was a very exciting match and the sheep were on the edge of their seats by the time the final point was scored and the best player won. The sheep were so excited they ran onto the tennis court and started nibbling the grass!

The umpire looked very cross. He got down out of his chair and tried to shoo them away but the sheep just ran about all over the place. Farmer John had to come and sort them out! Eventually he got them to behave themselves and bought them all strawberries and cream to keep them quiet.

By the time they got back to where they had parked Lawrence, they were all tired out. There was a big policeman standing by the Landrover.

'Is this your vehicle, sir?' he said to Farmer John.

'Yes, officer,' said Farmer John, 'it is.'

'You can't park here,' said the policeman, 'it's on double yellow lines. I'm going to have to give you a ticket, I'm afraid.'

'But we're from Thistledown Farm!' cried Farmer John.

'In that case, sir,' said the policeman, 'why didn't you say so? Everyone's heard of Thistledown Farm, it's a pleasure to meet you, Mr. Stubblefield. I'm sorry if I've caused you any inconvenience.'

'Don't mention it,' said Farmer John. 'Here.' And he gave the policeman a strawberry. It was a bit squashed, though, as it had been in his pocket!

Farmer John loaded up his sheep and drove off home. They were very pleased when they got back. They told all the other animals about everything they'd done, and the other animals were very interested to hear what the sheep had got up to, especially the escalators!

Farmer John gave the sheep their dinner. 'Did you like London?' he asked.

'Yees,' bleated the sheep, 'it was good fun, but we don't think we'd like to live there all the time. Everyone's in such a hurry and there aren't any fields. We've decided we prefer to live in the country. Thistledown Farm is the place for us.'

Farmer John smiled. 'I'm glad,' he said. 'You're right, London's exciting but Thistledown Farm is the place to be.' And he toddled back to the farmhouse for his tea.

FARMER JOHN'S PAYING GUESTS

Farmer John takes in some Paying Guests but things are not as they seem...

It was a bright winter's morning on Thistledown Farm and Farmer John was munching his breakfast with Wendy his wife.

'Why don't we go on holiday,' he said suddenly. 'I'm fed up with working so hard and you're always working too. We could do with a break. Where could we go?'

'I'd like to go to Spain,' said Wendy. 'It's nice and hot there, I could spend all day reading my book on the beach.'

'That would be good,' said Farmer John, 'and I could visit lots of Spanish farms to see what they do. They grow oranges over there, you know.'

'I don't think you could grow oranges here,' said Wendy. 'It's too cold. Anyway, we can't go, we haven't got enough money.'

'We could borrow some,' said Farmer John.

'But we've borrowed too much already,' said Wendy. 'The bank manager won't let us have any more.'

'Oh dear,' said Farmer John, 'I was looking forward to going on holiday. Never mind. 'He sat and read the farming paper. Suddenly he had an idea. 'Look,' he said to Wendy, 'there's an advert here for farmhouse holidays. People come and stay with you in the farmhouse and pay you for it. Why can't we do that? We could use the money to go on holiday!'

'Hmm,' said Wendy.' I'm not sure I like that idea.'

'Go on,' said Farmer John, 'it would be worth it if it meant we could afford a holiday. Let's advertise.'

'Oh, OK,' said Wendy, 'but only until we get enough money to go away, I don't want people staying in our house all the time.'

So Farmer John put an advert in the paper for Thistledown Farm holidays and it wasn't long before he had a booking. 'I've got two people coming tomorrow,' he said to Wendy. 'Now, let's try and be nice to them and make their stay comfortable, otherwise we won't get our money.'

Next day a man and a woman turned up at the farmyard in a blue car.

'Hello,' said Farmer John, 'you must be Mr and Mrs Smith – welcome to Thistledown Farm.'

'Can I use your toilet?' said the man.

'I need a shower,' said the woman, 'our bags are in the car.' And they marched into the house.

Farmer John was a little taken aback. 'How rude,' he muttered to himself. 'What do they think I am, some sort of slave?' He collected all their bags and suitcases and tottered into the house.

'Now I've put you in our nicest room,' he said to the man as he lugged everything up the stairs. 'I think you'll like it.' He opened the door.

'It's a bit small,' said the man, 'haven't you anything bigger?'

'But this is our biggest room,' said Farmer John.

'It'll have to do then,' said the man, sitting on the bed and bouncing up and down. 'This bed is a bit saggy,' he complained. 'I have a bad back, I need a hard bed to sleep on.'

Farmer John scratched his chin. 'I'll put a board under the mattress for you,' he said helpfully, 'that'll make it better.'

The man frowned. 'What time do you serve breakfast?'

'Whenever you get up,' said Farmer John.

'I'm an early riser,' said the man. 'I always get up at four-thirty.'

'Four-thirty!' cried Farmer John. 'Even *I* don't get up that early.'

'Is that a problem?' said the man nastily.

'No, no' said Farmer John hastily, 'not at all, anything to oblige.'

'We'd like some dinner brought up to us,' continued the man. 'Nothing special, just boiled eggs and toast, one done for three and a half minutes with the toast lightly browned, and one done for six minutes with the toast well done.'

'Of course,' said Farmer John, 'no problem, back in a tick.'

He rushed downstairs to the kitchen. Wendy was cooking the dinner. 'I've got an order for boiled eggs and toast,' he said to Wendy. 'One done for six minutes with the toast well done and the other for three and a half minutes with the toast lightly browned.'

Wendy looked at him. 'Are you being funny?' she said.

'Not at all,' said Farmer John, 'and they want their breakfast at four-thirty tomorrow morning.'

Wendy laughed. 'They'll be lucky,' she said. 'What do they think this is, the Ritz Hotel?'

Farmer John was a bit alarmed. 'Come on, Wendy my dear,' he said, 'remember what I told you, we've got to make their stay as comfortable as possible or we won't be able to go on holiday.'

'Hmm,' said Wendy. 'I'm busy, you'll have to do the eggs and toast.'

Farmer John blinked. 'But I've got all the farm work to do,' he said.

'I don't care,' said Wendy, 'it was your idea and I've got a job and all the housework to do.'

'Oh, OK then,' said Farmer John grudgingly. 'Where are the eggs?'

He carefully timed the boiled eggs and made the toast and then took them upstairs on a tray. He had made little decorations out of the napkins. He knocked on the door.

'Come,' said a voice.

Farmer John balanced the tray on one hand and went in. 'Your eggs, sir,' said Farmer John.

'Huh,' said the man, 'about time! Did you have to wait for the hen to lay them?'

Farmer John bit his tongue. 'Will that be all, sir?'

'We need a hot water bottle,' said the man, 'we're very cold.'

Farmer John trudged back down the stairs. He boiled the kettle and filled a bottle. He looked at his watch, it was past his bedtime and he hadn't had his dinner yet. 'Oh dear,' he thought, 'I don't think I'm cut out to be a waiter!'

When he went back upstairs again the guests had finished their eggs. 'My egg was too hard,' said the man.

'And my egg was too soft,' said the woman.

'But I timed them perfectly,' said Farmer John.

'You must have given us the wrong ones,' said the man. 'Mrs Smith was supposed to have the hard one.'

'I'm very sorry, sir,' said Farmer John, grovelling, 'it won't happen again.'

'It had better not,' said the man. 'Now don't forget, breakfast, four-thirty sharp!'

Farmer John took the tray and went downstairs. He was tired and hungry. 'Come on, John,' said Wendy, 'it's time for bed, you've got an early start in the morning.'

'But where's my dinner?' cried Farmer John.

'It went cold,' said Wendy, 'so I threw it out.'

'Oh dear,' moaned Farmer John. 'I can't be bothered to make anything now, I think I'll just go to bed.'

Farmer John wriggled under the covers.

'Where's our hot water bottle?' said Wendy.

'I gave it to the guests,' said Farmer John.

'You idiot,' said Wendy. 'Now I'm going to be cold all night.'

Farmer John shut his eyes. He'd had enough. He was exhausted, and soon began to snore, 'zzzzzzzzz.'

When he woke up, sunlight was streaming through the curtains and someone was banging on the door. He dragged himself out and opened it. Mr Smith was there, looking very angry. 'Where's my breakfast?' he demanded. 'I've been waiting four hours!'

Farmer John groaned. 'I'm so sorry, sir, I must have overslept.'

The man tutted. 'Well, it's not good enough. We've got a long day today, we've got lots of sights to see – just make us some sandwiches and we can be going.'

Farmer John trudged downstairs in his pyjamas. He made them some jam sandwiches and put them in a box with a couple of apples. 'There you are,' he said. 'Have a nice day.'

Mr and Mrs Smith left without saying goodbye.

It was about mid-morning when PC Collar turned up in the yard in his smart police car. He squeezed himself out. 'Morning, John,' he said. 'Can I have a word?'

'Of course,' said Farmer John. 'What's up?'

'There've been a lot of burglaries in the neighbourhood,' said PC Collar. 'Have you seen these suspects?'

Farmer John looked at the photographs in surprise. 'It's Mr and Mrs Smith,' he said, 'they're staying with us in the farmhouse.'

PC Collar tutted. 'They're not Mr and Mrs Smith,' he said, 'they're Soapy Sam and Slippery Sue, the jewel thieves. We've been looking for them for some time.'

'WHAT!' cried Farmer John. 'You mean Mr and Mrs Smith are crooks?'

'Yes,' said PC Collar, 'there's a reward for their capture.'

'Really?' said Farmer John. 'How exciting.'

'Let's have a look at their room,' said PC Collar.

They climbed the stairs. 'In here,' said Farmer John.

PC Collar went in. 'Hmm,' he said, 'let's see what's in this suitcase.' He flipped the latch. It was full of sparkling jewels.

'Oh my goodness!' cried Farmer John. 'What a hoard, and to think I was treating them like lords. What a fool I've been!'

'You weren't to know,' said PC Collar, 'but I think we need to make a few plans …'

That evening Soapy Sam and Slippery Sue arrived in the yard. They looked around. 'Everything seems to be all right,' they said. 'Let's have some more fun with that farmer.' They went up to their room. Everything was as they'd left it.

'We'll have dinner in our room again tonight,' said Soapy Sam when he saw Farmer John.

'Fine,' said Farmer John. 'Would you like to take advantage of our laundry service?'

'Thank you,' said Soapy Sam, 'that's a good idea. Here, take all our clothes but make sure we get them back clean and dry in the morning.'

'Of course, sir,' said Farmer John, smiling. 'No problem at all.' He went out with all their clothes and locked the door behind him.

Soapy Sam looked at Slippery Sue. 'Did you hear that? He's locked the door, what's he playing at? Oi!' he cried and banged on the door. 'Let us out!'

Farmer John laughed on the other side. 'You can stay there till the police come,' he said, 'the game's up!' He went downstairs and rang PC Collar. 'They're locked in their bedroom without any clothes,' he said. 'Are you going to come and pick them up?'

'Well done, John,' said the policeman. 'I'll be over right away.'

PC Collar raced into the yard with his blue light flashing. Soapy Sam and Slippery Sue were climbing down a drainpipe in their underwear. He put the handcuffs on them. '**GOTCHA!**' he cried. 'I arrest you in the name of the law.' He bundled them into the back of the police car.

Farmer John laughed as they were driven away. 'I knew there was something fishy about those two all along,' he said.

'Oh yes?' said Wendy, 'Is that why you were treating them like royalty?'

'Huh,' said Farmer John. 'There's one thing, though – now they've been arrested we won't get the money to go on holiday.'

'But what about the reward?' said Wendy.

'Of course,' cried Farmer John. 'One thousand pounds, what a fool I am!'

So Farmer John paid for a holiday out of his reward money and took Wendy and his family on holiday to Spain. He had to pay for someone else to look after his animals but they didn't mind, and when he came back he had brought some little orange trees with him.

All the animals held a big welcome home party because although they had been treated well while he was away, they were glad to see Farmer John back on Thistledown Farm again.

FARMER JOHN'S BEAUTY CONTEST

Farmer John holds a contest to see which of his animals is the most beautiful...

It was evening on Thistledown Farm and Farmer John had his feet up in front of the telly. Wendy his wife came in.

'What are you watching John?' she asked.

'It's Miss World,' said Farmer John. 'What a lot of beautiful girls there are, but none as beautiful as you, my dear.'

'Ha!' Wendy laughed. 'Do you really mean it?' she said.

'Of course,' said Farmer John. 'My wife's prettier to me than anyone else in the world.'

Wendy gave Farmer John a kiss. 'You say the sweetest things,' she said, 'but sometimes I think you love your animals more than me.'

'Well,' said Farmer John, 'my animals *are* pretty. My cows are the most beautiful herd in the county, my pigs are the cutest in the district and my sheep are the sweetest flock that anyone could hope to have.'

'I bet you've got your favourites,' said Wendy. 'Who is the most beautiful animal on the farm?'

Farmer John scratched his chin. 'I don't really know,' he said. 'I haven't thought about it before.'

'Why don't you have a competition,' said Wendy, 'to find out?'

'What a good idea,' said Farmer John, 'and the winner can ride a Thistledown Farm float at the autumn carnival. She can be the Thistledown Farm beauty queen!'

'That's a good idea,' said Wendy. 'I'll help you.'

So next morning Farmer John and Wendy got all the animals together and told them about the beauty contest. They were very excited.

'MOOO,' said Daisy. 'I've never been in a beauty contest before but I'm sure I'd win, I've got such gorgeous long eyelashes.'

'OINK,' said Suzie, 'I've got a naturally curly tail, I'm sure I'd win.'

'BAAA,' bleated Mavis, 'my fleece is so soft and snowy white, I'm bound to win.'

Farmer John laughed. 'Now now,' he said. 'You all look beautiful to me. The competition's to see who is the *most* beautiful and beauty is not just skin deep, it's about character and personality as well, you know.'

'I've got a lot of character,' said Suzie.

'So have I,' said Mavis.

'I have a captivating personality,' boasted Daisy. 'I know lots of stories.'

'I'm sure you do,' laughed Farmer John, 'but the competition's open to everyone on the farm, it's not just for you three.'

Wendy sat down and opened a book. 'Now then, all those who want to take part must come and register with me,' she said, and everyone crowded round. She took all their names and put them in a hat. She shook it up and drew out the first name. 'SUZIE THE SOW,' she announced. Suzie stepped forward.

'Right,' said Wendy. 'I'm going to ask you a few questions. Are you ready?'

'Oh yes,' said Suzie.

'Who is the best farmer in the county?'

Suzie puzzled for a moment then said, 'Farmer John, of course.'

'Very good,' said Wendy. 'Now, what would you do if you found a ten-pound note on the ground?'

Suzie puzzled. 'Someone would have dropped it,' she said. 'I'd hand it in to Farmer John.'

'Very good,' said Wendy.

'What's brown and sticky?'

Suzie laughed. 'A stick!'

'Well done,' said Wendy. 'Next question. Where does the sun rise in the morning?'

'In the east,' said Suzie.

'Very good,' said Wendy. 'How do you get an elephant in a telephone box?'

Suzie thought for a moment. 'With difficulty,' she said.

Wendy laughed. 'That's right. Now tell me,' she added, 'why do you want to be a beauty queen?'

'Well I think I'd do a lot of good work and be an ambassador for the farm,' Suzie replied.

Wendy was impressed. 'Do you have any hobbies?' she asked.

'I like collecting acorns,' answered Suzie.

'OK,' said Wendy. 'Final question. Has anything interesting happened to you lately?'

'Oh yes,' said Suzie. 'I went to the county show and had a ride on a big wheel and had my fortune told and feasted on cream cakes and won the show-jumping competition.'

'Goodness!' laughed Wendy. 'You did have a good time. OK, that's all for now, we'll let you know if you get through.'

Wendy called out all the animals' names and they all answered her questions. Finally only Daisy and Mavis were left.

'What would you do if you found a ten-pound note on the ground?' Wendy asked Mavis.

'Keep it,' replied Mavis. 'It would come in handy for a rainy day.'

'Hmm,' said Wendy.

'What's brown and sticky?'

'Treacle,' replied Mavis.

'Hmm,' said Wendy. 'I suppose you're right. How do you get an elephant in a telephone box?'

'With a shoehorn,' replied Mavis.

Wendy laughed. 'Why do you want to be beauty queen?' she asked.

'Because I am the most beautiful animal on the farm,' replied Mavis, 'and if I'm not picked it would be a miscarriage of justice.'

'Oh,' said Wendy, 'and has anything interesting happened to you lately?'

'I've been stolen by sheep rustlers,' said Mavis. 'It was really exciting.'

'Goodness,' said Wendy, 'you do lead an interesting life. OK, we'll let you know about the outcome.'

Daisy was last.

'Who is the best farmer in the county?'

'Oh I think Brian next door is the best farmer,' said Daisy. 'Nothing ever goes wrong on his farm.'

'Oh,' said Wendy. 'What's brown and sticky?'

'A cow pat!' said Daisy.

'Oh dear,' said Wendy. 'Where does the sun rise in the morning?'

'In the sky,' said Daisy.

'Well I suppose you're right,' said Wendy. 'How do you get an elephant in a telephone box?'

'By using lots of butter,' said Daisy.

Wendy laughed. 'Yes, that would work I suppose, it's very slippery. Why do you want to be beauty queen?'

'Because I think I would look so fine on top of that carnival float and everyone else would look up to me.'

'Hmmm. That *is* a reason, I suppose, but a little selfish perhaps,' thought Wendy.

'And finally, has anything interesting happened to you lately?'

'Oh yes,' said Daisy. 'I won the Dairy Cow Dash at the Thistledown Farm Olympics. We had a race and I came in first, it was my crowning moment.'

'My,' said Wendy, 'what an exciting life our animals do lead. OK, that's all for now, we'll let you know in due course.'

Farmer John and Wendy put their heads together. 'I think,' said Farmer John, 'that my animals are all as beautiful as each other. The only thing we can use to decide on is the interview.'

'I agree,' said Wendy. 'Who do you think should win?'

'Well, said Farmer John, 'I think it's between Daisy, Suzie and Mavis. I don't think Mavis was as honest as she could have been, she would have kept that ten-pound note for herself.'

'Yes,' said Wendy. 'I think that rather rules her out, I'm afraid.'

Farmer John nodded. 'And I think that Daisy's answer about why she wanted to be beauty queen was a bit selfish. I don't think *she* deserves the prize.'

Wendy was in agreement. 'Suzie answered all the questions well,' she said. 'She showed the best character and personality, I think she ought to win.'

'That's it then,' said Farmer John. 'We're decided.'

So Suzie the sow won the contest and that autumn, she got all dressed up and rode the carnival float through town. Everyone cheered and threw flowers at her and she blushed and giggled in delight.

Daisy and Mavis were a bit disappointed but when they were told why they hadn't won they had to admit to their mistakes.

Everyone enjoyed the beauty contest so much that Farmer John decided to hold one every year and from then on, at carnival time, the Thistledown Farm Beauty Queen became the centre of attraction.

FARMER JOHN'S WEDDING

Farmer John is getting married but will he get to the Church on time?

It was a bright spring morning on Thistledown Farm and Farmer John was up and about milking his cows. 'What lovely weather,' he said. 'It's a nice day for a wedding.' And he began to sing a little song: 'I'm getting married in the morning!'

The cows were very interested. 'Are you getting married, John?' they asked.

'Yes,' said Farmer John. 'It's my wedding day. Wendy and I are getting married this afternoon, isn't it great.'

The cows were very excited. 'We love weddings,' they said. 'Can we come too?'

'Oh yes,' said Farmer John. 'Everyone's invited, it's going to be a very big do.'

'Brilliant,' said the cows. 'We'll have to find something to wear. What are you wearing, John?'

'I'm going to wear top hat and tails,' said Farmer John. 'I'm going to the tailor's this morning to pick them up.' He finished the milking and washed the parlour down. 'Ding dong the bells are going to chime,' he sang as he hosed the floor. 'Get me to the church on time!'

He put away the hose and went in for his breakfast. Wendy wasn't around. 'It's bad luck for a man to see his bride before the wedding,' he thought. He fried some bacon and eggs and sat down to eat. He looked at his watch – it was still early. 'Plenty of time,' he said to himself, 'things are going well but I must be careful, I don't want to be late.' He washed up his plate and sat down to read his newspaper.

'Marriages, Marriages, Marriages,' he said. 'Ah, here we are. *The wedding takes place today between Wendy Sweetlove and John Stubblefield, 2pm at St. Elsewheres Church, Dexeter. Reception afterwards at Thistledown Farm.*'

He looked at his watch again. It was ten o'clock. 'I ought to be off to the tailor's,' he thought, but just then an article in the paper caught his eye. It was about sheep. 'How interesting,' he said, and he began to read. He read and he read and he read. Then he saw something about cows. He read that too.

When he had finished he turned the page. There was a piece about pigs. 'Hmm, I wonder what that says,' he thought, and he carried on reading.

It wasn't long before the clock chimed twelve! Farmer John looked up. 'Oh my goodness!' he cried.

'It's midday, I've got to be at the church by two and I haven't collected my suit yet! I'd better get going.'

He jumped up and dashed out of the door. He climbed into Lawrence the Landrover and hurried off down the road to see the tailor. He marched into the shop. 'I need my suit,' he said, 'I'm late.'

The tailor looked at him. 'I'm sorry, sir, but we need to measure you first.'

'I haven't got time for that,' said Farmer John. 'Any old suit will do and don't forget the hat, I must have a hat.'

The tailor grabbed a suit from the rack and handed it over. He found a grey top hat and gave it to Farmer John. 'There we are, sir, that should be all right, and may I offer you my heartiest congratulations...' But Farmer John had vanished. He threw his suit and hat onto Lawrence's seat and raced back home.

When he got back it was one o'clock. 'There's still plenty of time,' he said to himself. 'I'd better have some lunch.' But he didn't feel very hungry, he was a bit nervous. He made himself a little sandwich.

'There,' he said, 'that's better. Now I ought to try on my suit.'

He went upstairs. He pulled on his trousers and tailcoat. They were a bit baggy. The sleeves were too long and the trousers were far too big. He found a piece of baler twine and tied them up with that. 'There,' he said, 'and now for the hat.' He picked up the grey topper. It looked very nice. He put it on his head. It was a bit big too and came down over his ears.

'Oh dear,' he said. 'Never mind, it'll have to do.' He looked at his watch. It was half past one. 'Plenty of time,' he said. Then he jumped. 'Help,' he cried, 'I haven't fed my animals!'

He rushed downstairs and pulled on his wellies. He dashed out across the yard but halfway he slipped on a cow pat and fell in a pile of manure. 'Oh bother,' he said, 'now I've got a mucky bottom.' He walked up to the sheep shed brushing his baggy trousers. Mavis the ewe was at the water trough.

'Hello, John,' she said, 'I didn't recognise you in your wedding suit. It's a bit big, isn't it, and what have you done to your trousers?'

'I had an accident,' said Farmer John. 'Here, you'd better have some hay' and he gave Mavis a bale. He got covered in bits of hay as he put it in the rack.

At the pig-pens Suzie the sow was scratching herself on the wall. 'Goodness, John,' she said. 'You're not going to your wedding looking like that, are you?'

'Don't fuss,' said Farmer John. 'Here, have some straw', and he bedded the pigs down. He got rather covered in straw himself and he left the pigs looking like a smart scarecrow.

Daisy the dairy cow was a bit taken aback when Farmer John arrived. 'What *doo* you look like, John?' she said. 'You've got a mucky bottom and you're covered in hay and straw! You'd better get cleaned up before you go to church.'

Farmer John looked at his watch. 'I haven't got time,' he said. 'It's two o'clock, I'm late already.' And he gave Daisy her food, jumped into Lawrence the Landrover and dashed off.

At the church people were waiting. Some of his cows were sitting in the pews wearing big brightly coloured hats. People were coughing politely and craning their necks. 'Where's the groom?' they whispered to each other.

Poor Wendy was standing alone at the altar. She looked very beautiful in her wedding dress.

Suddenly Farmer John came bursting in. Everyone turned to look at him. What a sight! He was wearing a suit that was far too big for him, and a top hat that was down over his ears. He was wearing a pair of mucky green Wellingtons and he was covered in hay and straw!

He marched down the aisle and stood next to Wendy. The vicar turned up his nose. 'Bless my soul, John,' he said, 'what an unholy smell! What *have* you been doing?'

'I'm sorry,' said Farmer John. 'I lost track of time.'

'Well, we'd better get on,' said the vicar. 'Dearly beloved, we are gathered here today to witness the marriage of John and Wendy.' Everyone fanned themselves, there was a very rich pong in the air!

'Do you, Wendy Sweetlove, take John Stubblefield to be your lawful wedded husband?' said the vicar.

Wendy looked at Farmer John. She smiled. 'Yes,' she said, 'I do.'

'Do you, John Stubblefield, take Wendy Sweetlove to be your lawful wedded wife?' said the vicar.

Farmer John looked at Wendy. 'I do,' he said very loudly.

'I now pronounce you man and wife,' said the vicar. 'You may kiss the bride.' Wendy lifted her veil. Farmer John kissed her. The congregation beamed.

Farmer John shook the vicar's hand. 'Cleanliness is next to godliness, John,' said the vicar disapprovingly.

Farmer John looked down at his mucky wellies. 'But where there's muck there's money!' he said. The vicar laughed.

Outside, Tommy the tractor was waiting. He had white ribbons tied on his bonnet and a sign saying 'Just

Married' tied to his cab. Farmer John sat in the driving seat and Wendy perched next to him. They drove off with a clatter; someone had tied some old tin cans to Tommy's draw-bar with string.

Everyone went back to Thistledown Farm for the reception. There was a huge marquee in the big field and they had music and champagne. Wendy and Farmer John cut a big cake with little toy farm animals on the top and Farmer John made a speech. 'I knew Wendy was the girl for me the first time I set eyes on her,' he said. Wendy blushed.

The band started to play and everyone got up to dance. The pigs danced with the cows, the cows danced with the sheep and the sheep danced with the pigs, and they all had a great time.

Wendy and Farmer John slipped away. 'I think we'll leave them all to enjoy themselves,' said Farmer John.

'Yes,' said Wendy, 'you ought to change out of those smelly clothes and I'm a bit tired. Let's have an early night.'

'Good idea,' said Farmer John. 'I've got cows to milk in the morning. Come here, wife!' And they gave each other a huge kiss.

FARMER JOHN'S COMEUPPANCE

Farmer John decides it's time to deal with his sheep but it isn't long before *they* are dealing with him!

One bright morning Farmer John jumped out of bed and looked at his calendar. 'It's time I did something with those sheep,' he said to Wendy his wife.

'But you're *always* doing something to your sheep!' said Wendy. 'They're so much trouble. They're always getting out or falling ill. Can't you keep something easier to manage?'

'But I like my sheep,' said Farmer John, 'My flock are the prettiest in the county. My ewes are cute and cuddly and my lambs are the sweetest little things. They're so good-natured they don't mind all the things I have to do to them.'

'What are you going to do to them today?' asked Wendy.

'Well, first I'm going to worm them,' said Farmer John, 'then I'm going to trim their toenails, then I'm going to dip them and when I've done all that I'm going to shear them.'

'Goodness,' laughed Wendy, 'you *are* going to be busy today! I won't bother making you any lunch, you won't have time.'

Farmer John frowned. 'But I need to eat,' he said. 'Can't you give me anything?'

Wendy smiled. 'Perhaps I could make you a few sandwiches,' she said, 'if you're good.'

'That would be nice,' said Farmer John, relieved. 'I'll need all my strength if I'm going to be dealing with sheep all day.'

He dressed and went downstairs for breakfast. When he had finished he put on his boots and went to the workshop to get some sheep wormer. He tied the bottle of medicine to his back. A coil of tubing ran from the bottle to the dosing gun. Farmer John filled it by squeezing the trigger.

'Now I'm ready,' he said and marched off up to the sheep shed. The ewes were standing in the pens. 'Here he comes,' said Mavis. 'What's he going to do to us now? Oh no, he's got the dosing gun! Look out, girls, it's medicine time!'

Farmer John climbed over the hurdles and grabbed a sheep. 'Baa,' it went, and Farmer John slipped the dosing gun's nozzle into its mouth. He squeezed the trigger and a squirt of medicine shot down the sheep's throat. 'Yeuk!' said the sheep and tried to spit the medicine out, but Farmer John held its mouth shut. She swallowed.

'There,' said Farmer John, 'that's you done.'

'Baa,' said the sheep, 'what a horrible taste!'

'Don't moan,' said Farmer John, 'it's good for you!'

Farmer John worked his way through the sheep. By the time he had finished they were looking very fed up. 'Thank goodness that's over,' they said. 'Perhaps we can have some peace now!'

But it wasn't long before Farmer John was back. He had Shep the sheepdog with him. 'Baa,' said the sheep, 'look out, he's up to something else now!'

Shep chased the sheep up a long race and Farmer John stood at the end by a turnover crate. Mavis the ewe ran into the strange contraption. Farmer John pulled a lever and WOAH!, Mavis spun around upside down, her legs waving in the air. Farmer John grabbed a leg, took some clippers and began to trim Mavis's toenails.

'Baa,' said Mavis, 'I suppose you think this is funny!'

'Don't worry, Mavis,' said Farmer John. 'I won't be long.'

He trimmed all Mavis's hooves and let her go. She was a bit dizzy from being upside down.

'Blooming farmer, can't he leave us alone?' grumbled Mavis. Farmer John trimmed all the sheep's toenails then got a hose and filled the sheep dip.

'Look out,' said the sheep, 'we're going for a swim now!'

The sheep slipped one by one into the dip and swam round and round, coughing and spluttering. They hauled themselves out into the draining pen, dripping with water. Farmer John laughed at them. 'You won't have any trouble with lice and ticks now,' he said.

'Baa,' the sheep went. 'First you give us nasty medicine, then you turn us all upside down and then, as if we haven't had enough, you try to drown us all!'

Farmer John laughed. 'I haven't finished with you yet,' he said. 'When you've dried out I'm going to shear you.'

'But we like our woolly coats,' the sheep bleated.

'You may do,' said Farmer John, 'but they're getting too shaggy, it's time you had a hair cut.'

Farmer John got his sheep shears out and plugged the machine in. He pulled a switch and the shears started to buzz. He grabbed a sheep and began to clip all the wool off its back. The sheep struggled and wriggled and Farmer John started to sweat. Suddenly, without any warning, the whole flock surrounded Farmer John on the shearing boards. They were looking very menacing.

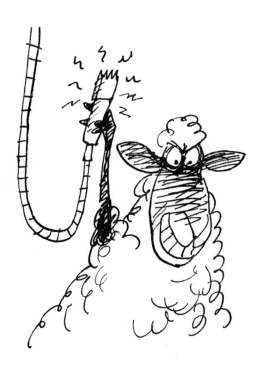

'We've had enough of being pushed around all the time,' they said. 'See how you like it for a change – come on girls!' And they grabbed the clippers from Farmer John's hand and knocked him over and sat on him. Mavis took the clippers and began to shave all the hair off Farmer John's head.

'STOP, STOP!' he cried but it was no use. The sheep were getting their own back. It wasn't long before there was a pile of Farmer John's black hair on the floor.

'Right,' said the sheep, 'what can we do next?'

'Trim his toenails,' said Mavis, so they carried him across to the turnover crate and popped him inside. Mavis pulled the lever and Farmer John spun over upside down. Mavis pulled off Farmer John's boots and socks and started clipping his long toenails.

'Ouch!' said Farmer John. 'Be careful.'

'Now you know how it feels for us,' laughed Mavis. Farmer John's toenails flew through the air.

'Now while you're in that position,' said Mavis, 'I think you should take your medicine.'

The sheep cheered. 'Yes! You need worming!'

'NO!' shouted Farmer John. 'I haven't got worms!'

'But you might have,' said Mavis. 'Now be a good boy, it won't hurt at all.' She got the dosing gun and squirted white worm medicine into Farmer John's mouth.

'Yeuk!' Farmer John spat it out. 'That is disgusting,' he said.

'So why do you give it to us then?' said Mavis.

'Because it's good for you,' said Farmer John.

'If it's good for us, it'll be good for you,' laughed Mavis.

'Now what else can we do with you. Of course, the dip!'

'Oh no,' Farmer John groaned, 'not the dip!'

'Yes you must,' said the sheep, 'if we have to do it, so do you.'

They grabbed Farmer John by his arms and legs and carried him across to the sheep dip. They dropped him in with a SPLOSH! Farmer John sank under the surface and came up coughing. He began to swim around and around. 'Let me out, let me out!' he cried, but the sheep weren't having any of it.

'You can swim around in there till you're free of ticks,' they said. 'You make us do it, now you see how it feels.'

Eventually they took pity on him and let him out. He came out sopping wet, his boots full of water and his clothes dripping.

'There,' said the sheep, 'perhaps you'll be a little more thoughtful when you do things to us in future, now you know what it's like to be a sheep.'

Farmer John nodded. 'Perhaps I'll only do one thing at a time in future,' he said, 'instead of trying to do everything in one day.'

'Baa,' the sheep bleated, 'that's a good idea. We don't mind taking our medicine or having our feet trimmed and being sheared and dipped, but all at once is a bit much.'

Farmer John squelched his way back to the farmhouse.

'Hello, dear,' said Wendy, 'how did it go?'

'Oh all right,' said Farmer John. 'I got most of it done but I got most of it done to me as well.'

Wendy laughed. 'It looks like it,' she said. 'I think you need a bath, and what's happened to your hair? It looks like you've had an accident with the lawnmower.'

Farmer John emptied his soggy boots and wrung out his wet socks. 'I'll say one thing,' he said, 'my sheep may be the prettiest in the county but when they get upset, they mean business!'

FARMER JOHN'S ROBOT

Farmer John is working too hard but his new robot goes badly wrong!

It was evening on Thistledown Farm and Farmer John was asleep in his armchair with the farming paper over his head. 'Zzzzzz…' He was tired. He had been working so hard that he couldn't even be bothered to go to bed.

He had to be up by six o'clock every morning to milk the cows, then feed them and the other animals. Then he had to spend all day driving Tommy his tractor, mowing grass. He had to shear his sheep and collect the eggs and then he had to milk the cows and feed the animals again in the evening before he could finally feed himself.

He snored loudly and woke himself up. 'What! Where am I?' he mumbled. 'Oh, I'm working too hard,' he groaned.

Wendy his wife looked at him. 'You're worn out,' she said, 'perhaps you should give up farming.'

'Give up farming!' said Farmer John. 'But what else would I do?'

'I don't know,' said Wendy, 'there must be easier ways to make a living.'

'Perhaps you're right,' said Farmer John, 'but what would happen to all my animals?'

'That's true,' said Wendy, 'we'll have to think of something else.'

Farmer John looked at his newspaper. Suddenly he sat up. 'Look at this,' he said to Wendy. He showed her a colourful advert with the words '*Control everything from the comfort of your armchair!*'

'The Haywire Engineering Company Ltd,' he read, 'is proud to announce its latest machine for overworked farmers – the fully automatic, all purpose farm hand, or Farmbot for short. Using up to the minute microchip technology combined with years of experience in making farm machinery, Haywire UK Ltd has produced a robot farm hand which will perform all known farming tasks, leaving the farmer free to pursue a lifetime of leisure!'

'It's a robot-computer,' said Farmer John to Wendy, 'it does all the work for you. That's just what I need!'

He jumped up and went to the telephone. When he came back he had a big smile on his face. 'I've just ordered the biggest and best Farmbot they had,' he said, rubbing his hands. 'Now I won't have to do a thing!' And he went off up to bed, chuckling to himself.

Next morning Pete the postman drove into the yard and Farmer John helped him unload a huge heavy box.

'There you are, John,' said Pete, 'Christmas has come early!'

'Yes,' said Farmer John 'it's my new robot, now I won't have to lift a finger!'

'Lucky old you,' laughed the postman, 'good luck!' And he drove off.

Farmer John wasted no time unwrapping his robot. It was a very strange looking contraption with lots of buttons and lights, levers and cogs and dials with tangles of wire poking out everywhere. It had three round eyes, two pairs of arms and a pair of legs. Farmer John couldn't be bothered to read the instructions, he couldn't make much sense of them 'Oh well,' he thought, 'it can't be that difficult.'

He began pushing the machine's buttons and suddenly the thing came to life. It jerked and lurched and chattered and began to wave its arms and legs around.

'Right,' said Farmer John. He put the machine in the middle of the farmyard, took the remote control and went back to the house and sat in his comfortable armchair. He pushed a button marked 'milk the cows', sat back and soon began to snore. 'Zzzzzzz...'

He woke up with a start. '**MOOOOO!**' There was a great hullabaloo coming from the direction of the milking parlour. 'Oh no,' groaned Farmer John, 'I haven't been asleep five minutes!' He jumped into his boots and rushed across the yard.

There was pandemonium in the milking shed. The cows were mooing at the top of their voices and dancing and jumping around. Farmer John could see what was wrong. The machine had stopped *milking* his cows and begun *tickling* them!

'OH NO!' he cried and pushed a button marked 'stop'. The machine slowed down and came to rest. 'Oh dear,' thought Farmer John, 'what a disaster! I'd better finish the milking myself.' But the cows were so upset that they wouldn't give any more milk. Farmer John went back to the house.

'You're early, dear,' said Wendy.

'I don't want to talk about it,' said Farmer John.

He sank into his armchair. 'Right,' he said, 'now let's see about those chickens.' He pushed a button on the remote control marked 'Collect the eggs'.

'There,' he said, 'that should be OK. Now for some sleep…Zzzzzz…'

'**AAAARGH!**' He was woken by screaming coming from the kitchen. He jumped up in alarm. His machine was standing at the door, pelting Wendy with eggs. She was plastered from head to foot in sticky egg yolk.

'STOP! STOP!' he yelled but the machine just started lobbing eggs in his direction! Farmer John stepped forward but slipped on egg on the floor and landed OUCH! on his bottom! He grabbed the remote control and stopped the crazy contraption. Poor Farmer John, Wendy wasn't very happy with him at all!

'JOHN STUBBLEFIELD,' she cried, 'take that horrible machine away at once!' She was very cross with Farmer John.

Farmer John took his machine and put it in Tommy the tractor's cab. 'There,' he said, 'now you can mow the grass while I have a nice long sleep.' He took the remote control and collapsed in his armchair. He pushed a button marked 'Drive the tractor' and soon nodded off.

It wasn't long before he was woken again. Tommy was driving round and round the yard chasing the chickens!

Farmer John stood in the middle of the yard. His machine drove straight at him and he had to jump for his life. He landed SQUELCH in a pile of manure. Farmer John got up covered in dung.

'POOH!' he said. 'What a stink! Botheration.' He pushed the stop button on his remote control and Tommy came to a stop. Farmer John pulled his machine out. He was very angry. 'Right,' he said, 'I'm giving you one last chance.' He pushed a button that said 'Shear the sheep' and the machine clanked off up to the sheep shed. Farmer John went home for a nap. 'Perhaps *now* I can get some sleep,' he said. 'Zzzzzz…'

But it wasn't long before he was woken yet again.

'**BAAAAA!**' He ran up to the sheep shed. The machine was giving every sheep a poodle haircut!

'STOP, STOP!' cried Farmer John but the machine grabbed hold of him and began to shave his eyebrows off! 'NO, NO, NO,' he shouted, 'put me down!'

Poor Farmer John, he hadn't had much of a rest! He was a bit fed up. He trudged back to the farmhouse where Wendy was waiting for him.

'Goodness John,' she said, 'what's happened to you?'

'I got a free haircut,' said Farmer John gloomily. 'That machine's useless, it won't do what it's told. It's tickled my cows, smashed all my eggs, scared my chickens and made my sheep look even sillier than usual. Worse than that, I'm covered in dung, you're covered in egg yolk and I've got no eyebrows left!'

Wendy laughed 'Oh dear,' she said, 'we haven't had a very good day, have we?

Farmer John suddenly had a bright idea. 'I know what that robot will be good at,' he said and he rushed upstairs and came down with some old clothes. He dressed his robot up in a coat and a hat and put it in his cornfield. 'There,' he said, 'you'll make a very good scarecrow!' The machine clanked around and was soon scaring off the birds.

'So you don't think we should give up farming then?' said Wendy when he got back to the farmhouse.

Farmer John looked shocked. 'But I enjoy it,' he said, 'it's my life. I'd never do anything else. I don't really mind having to work hard for a living because life on Thistledown Farm is never dull!'

Wendy laughed. 'You're right there,' she said and they gave each other a huge hug!

FARMER JOHN'S PIGS' BREAKFAST

Farmer John's Pigs are eating him out of house and home but his home-made pigswill doesn't go down very well...

It was early morning on Thistledown Farm and Farmer John was sitting having his breakfast. 'My pigs are eating too much,' he complained to Wendy his wife. 'It's costing me a fortune.'

'Oh dear,' said Wendy. 'If we're not careful we'll be eaten out of house and home.'

'You're right,' said Farmer John. 'I need to put my thinking cap on.' And he pulled on his wellies and went out into the yard.

The pigs were making a huge row when he arrived at the pig-pens. 'WHEEE!' they all went. 'Where's our breakfast? We're starving!'

Farmer John looked at them. He was a little scared, they looked like they would eat *him* up if they got the chance! He decided to give them what they wanted. He emptied a big bag of expensive pig food into the trough and they all rushed to gobble it up. Farmer John was glad to be on the other side of the wall!

Farmer John left the pigs and went over to the cow yard. Daisy was standing by the water trough. 'Mooo,' she said. 'Morning John, how are you today?'

'Oh, I'm OK,' said Farmer John, 'but I'm a bit worried about my pigs. If they keep on eating like this I won't have any money left to buy food for you.'

Daisy was alarmed. 'But surely that won't happen?' she said.

'You never know,' said Farmer John, 'but don't worry, I'm sure I'll think of something,' and he left Daisy and toddled off up to the sheep shed.

Mavis the ewe was chewing some hay when he arrived. 'Morning, Mavis,' said Farmer John. 'How are you today?'

'Baa,' said Mavis, 'not baad, and yourself?'

'Oh, I don't know,' said Farmer John. 'I'm a bit worried about my pigs, they're eating too much. If I don't do something soon I'm going to be out of business.'

'Baa,' said Mavis, 'you need to feed them something cheaper, John.'

'Like what?' said Farmer John.

'What about leftovers?' suggested Mavis.

'Leftovers,' said Farmer John. 'Hmmm, what a good idea, why didn't I think of that? Thank you, Mavis.' And he ran back to the farmhouse to find Wendy.

'Wendy!' he cried. 'I've had an idea.'

'Oh yes,' said Wendy, 'what's that then?'

'Have you got any leftovers from the kitchen to save for the pigs?'

'Oh yes,' said Wendy, 'I've got lots. I've got potato peelings, I've got cabbage leaves, I've got bread crusts, I've got stale toast and squashed tomatoes. I've got sour milk and apple cores and orange peel and banana skins and carrot tops and broken biscuits and hard cheese and green cider…'

'STOP, STOP!' laughed Farmer John. 'That sounds plenty to me. I'd better get some buckets to collect it all.'

Farmer John filled his buckets with all the slops and carried them across to the dairy. He topped up six churns with Wendy's pigswill. He was very pleased with himself.

'Those pigs will love this,' he grinned to himself, rubbing his hands, 'and it will be cheaper for me too.' He was very busy the rest of the day and that night when he went to bed, he had forgotten all about his hungry pigs.

When he woke up next morning he yawned and opened his eyes. It was still dark. He crawled out of bed and groped for his clothes. Wendy was still asleep, and he didn't want to wake her. In the porch he pulled on his wellies, then went out into the yard. He listened. It was very quiet. The pigs were still asleep.

He tiptoed across the yard to the dairy. He filled the buckets with swill and carried them down to the pig-pens. He quietly tipped up the buckets and emptied them into the trough. 'OINK!' The pigs woke up in an instant and came rushing out. They stuck their snouts in the trough but instead of gobbling up their breakfast, they lifted up their heads and looked at Farmer John.

'WHAT'S THIS?!' they complained. 'This isn't our normal breakfast, what's happened to our nice pig food?'

Farmer John laughed. 'This is what you're having from now on,' he said. 'It's called a balanced diet. You'll soon get used to it.'

'But we can't eat this,' complained Suzie the sow. 'It's horrible, we deserve much better.'

Farmer John laughed. 'I'm sorry,' he said. 'Beggars can't be choosers. Now you'd better tuck in or you'll go hungry.'

The pigs left their breakfast in the trough. 'If we don't eat it, Farmer John will have to give us our proper food,' they said, and sat in the straw and grumbled.

Farmer John was a bit worried about his pigs. They didn't seem to like his new breakfast at all. 'What am I going to do with all this swill?' he muttered to himself. 'My pigs won't eat it. Perhaps I could find a use for it somewhere.' He scratched his chin.

Just then a car drove into the yard. A man got out. He was dressed in white with a chef's hat on his head. 'Excuse me, monsieur,' he said, 'but can you tell me where I am? I'm trying to find an hotel hereabouts but now I'm completely lost.'

Farmer John jumped up. 'Are you a chef?' he asked.

'Yes,' said the man. 'I am Gordon Ronay, ze greatest chef zat ever lived!'

Farmer John grabbed him. 'Come with me,' he said.

The chef followed Farmer John to the dairy. 'Can you make my pigs eat this?' he asked.

'Of course,' said the chef. 'I am ze greatest, no-one turns up zeir nose at my food, I have ze five stars at all my restaurants.'

The chef whisked up all the ingredients and cooked them with handfuls of herbs and spices. 'Zees ees my zeecret recipe,' he said to Farmer John, 'but you can have it for nuzzink.'

Farmer John was delighted. He poured the breakfast into the pigs' troughs and they sniffed the air. They were soon tucking in like Trojans.

'Thanks ever so much,' said Farmer John. 'Whatever can I do to repay you?'

'Oh, nuzzink,' said the chef. 'It is my pleasure to help you, Monsieur Stubblefield.' Farmer John directed the chef to his hotel and he drove off with a wave.

Farmer John was so proud of his pigswill that from then on he hung a sign at the end of his lane saying

'Thistledown Farm – Five Star Pigs' Breakfasts', and none of his pigs complained ever again!

FARMER JOHN'S BOOK

Everyone on the farm has their nose in a book but Farmer John's book isn't the best of bedtime reading!

One morning Farmer John was having breakfast with Wendy his wife. 'What are you reading, my dear,' he asked.

'A book,' said Wendy.

'I can see that,' said Farmer John. 'What's it called?'

'It's called *How to do a Hundred Things at Once* by Justin A Tick.'

'Ha!' laughed Farmer John. 'That sounds useful, I could do with reading that myself.'

'Why don't *you* read a book?' said Wendy. 'They're good for you.'

'What do you mean, good for you?' said Farmer John.

'They improve the mind,' said Wendy. 'Your mind could do with improving!'

'There's nothing wrong with *my* mind,' said Farmer John. 'Anyway, I haven't got time to read books, I'm too busy.' And he went out to feed his animals.

Daisy the dairy cow was lying down in the cow barn after milking. 'Morning, John,' she said, 'come and see this, I've found a really interesting book.'

'Oh yes,' said Farmer John, 'what's that then?'

'It's called *Produce More Milk* by Phil Churn,' said Daisy. 'Perhaps you might like to borrow it?'

'Hmm,' said Farmer John, 'sounds interesting but I haven't got time. I've got lots to do today.' And he gave all the cows some hay and went down to the pig-pens.

Suzie the sow was sitting in the straw. 'Morning, Suzie,' said Farmer John. 'What's that you're reading?'

'It's called *Know Your Pigs* by C Goodbacon,' said Suzie. 'It's very interesting, you might like to read it when I'm finished.'

'Maybe,' said Farmer John. 'I think I know quite a lot about pigs already but I might if I get time.' And he gave the pigs their sow nuts and pushed off to see the sheep.

Mavis the ewe was standing by the hurdles with a book propped up against the bars. 'Morning, Mavis,' said Farmer John,' don't say you're reading as well! Everyone seems to be at it this morning. What's your book called?'

'...ed *Sheep Keeping* by Baarbara Lamb,' said ...here's lots of things in it I didn't know, do ...want to see?'

'Yes,' said Farmer John, 'here's something new. It says that sheep are intelligent. I always thought they were rather silly.'

'Baa,' said Mavis, 'that's because you're stupid. We sheep are very clever, we know lots of things.'

'Well,' said Farmer John, 'you know how to read books, that's for sure. Perhaps I should do a bit of reading myself but where do I find a book?'

'Go to the library,' said Mavis, 'they have lots of books there. A travelling library comes to the village tomorrow, why not try that?'

So next day Farmer John went to the village with his library ticket. 'Morning!' he said to the librarian cheerfully.

'Ssh!' said the librarian, 'please be quiet! This is a library, not a farm!'

'Sorry,' said Farmer John sheepishly. 'Have you got any books?'

'Look around,' said the librarian. 'Books are ou. business.'

Farmer John looked through the shelves. There were lots of titles. 'Hmm,' he said as he read them all. '*Bee keeping* by B Hive, *Adventures on a Railway* by A Train, *Improve Your Eyesight* by C Well. Gosh,' he said, 'there's so many, how can I choose?' He looked again. 'Ah, here we are,' he said. 'Now, this sounds interesting, *How to Make a Lot of Money from Farming* by G E T Richquick. I must have this,' he thought.

The librarian stamped his book and he rushed out of the van and buzzed off home.

Wendy laughed when she saw him coming in with a book under his arm. 'I thought you said you didn't have time to read,' she said.

'Well,' said Farmer John, 'everyone else is reading so I thought I'd get myself a book and have a go. Look what I got.' And he showed Wendy the title.

'Hmm,' said Wendy. '*How to Make a Lot of Money from Farming*. That sounds good, we could do with a bit more to spend. You might pick up a few ideas.'

So that night when he went to bed, Farmer John started to read his book. Wendy had gone to sleep so he used a torch and read under the covers.

'To make money from farming,' the book said, 'you need to THINK BIG. You need to be a BIG farmer with BIG machines and grow LOTS of corn.' Farmer John scratched his chin. 'Hmm,' he thought and he carried on reading. 'Get rid of your animals,' the book said, 'and bulldoze all your hedges to make one HUGE field. Then plough it all up and plant wheat every year. You'll soon become very rich indeed and you can retire!'

Farmer John put his book down and fell asleep. He began to dream. He had sold all his animals and there was no-one on the farm. He was standing in the middle of a huge field of wheat without a hedge in sight. He was feeling very lonely. He tried to talk to his big machines but they were very unfriendly. Then he was suddenly surrounded by lots of wild animals and birds. 'What have you done with our homes?' they were saying to him. 'Where can we go now, we've got nowhere to live!'

Farmer John tossed and turned in his bed. The animals were tugging at his sleeves, saying, 'Help us, please help us!'

Suddenly he woke up. Wendy was pulling at his arm and shaking him. 'What's the matter, John?' she said.

'I must have been having a nightmare,' said Farmer John. 'It's that book, everything it tells you to do is rubbish. How could I get rid of all my animals and grow nothing but corn and throw all those lovely animals and birds out of their homes? It wouldn't be fair.'

'Goodness,' said Wendy, 'is that what you have to do to make a lot of money from farming? I don't think you ought to read any more of that book, it sounds horrid!'

'Yes,' said Farmer John, 'my way of farming is much better.'

Wendy had an idea. 'Why don't *you* write a book,' she said. 'You could call it *How To Be a Good Farmer*.'

'What a great idea,' said Farmer John.

So after breakfast next day he went into his office and closed the door. He got a piece of paper and began to write. He wrote and he wrote and he wrote. He put everything down that he knew. He had a chapter on how to milk a cow, another on how to shear a sheep and another on how to make good hay. He wrote furiously until his arm ached. Finally he put down his pen. 'Finished at last,' he said. 'There. *HOW TO BE A GOOD FARMER* by JOHN STUBBLEFIELD.' He looked at the first page. It said: 'WHAT YOU NEED:'

'A dog, a stick, a cap, a pair of gumboots, some sheep, some cows, some pigs, a few hens and a bit of land.' Then it said: 'WHAT YOU NEED TO DO:'

'Make hay in summer to feed your cows and sheep in winter, then grow grass to feed them the rest of the year. Grow some corn to sell and keep some to feed to your animals. It's as simple as that.'

Farmer John's book sold very well and soon every farmer in the country was reading it. Farmer John gave all his animals a signed copy and Daisy, Suzie and

Mavis had their photos on the front cover alongside a beaming Farmer John.

Wendy was very proud of her husband. 'Money's not everything, John,' she said. 'Looking after the countryside is important too.'

'Yes,' said Farmer John, 'as long as I know that I'm farming well and we all have enough to eat and drink, then John Stubblefield's a happy man!'

FARMER JOHN'S GHOST

**Farmer John and Wendy spend a freaky night
in by the fire...**

It was Halloween on Thistledown Farm and Farmer John had his feet up in front of the fire. The flames flickered merrily as he sipped a glass of ginger wine. He was nice and cosy and he snuggled up close to Wendy his wife.

'What a lovely evening,' he said. 'It's good to be snug and warm when it's dark and cold outside.'

'Yes,' said Wendy. 'Safe from all those ghoulies and ghosties out there.'

'Ghoulies and ghosties!' said Farmer John. 'What rubbish! Ghoulies and ghosties indeed! There's no such thing.'

Wendy laughed. 'You have to be in the right place at the right time if you want to see them,' she said.

'But I don't want to see them,' said Farmer John. 'Nasty, horrible, spooky things, I don't want anything to do with them. Anyway, they don't exist, so there.'

'You're not afraid of ghosts, are you?' said Wendy.

'Of course I'm not,' said Farmer John. 'They're a figment of your imagination. People just imagine they see them, that's all.'

'Really?' said Wendy. 'My Aunt Jessie she used to see ghosts all the time – her cottage was haunted, you know.'

'Rubbish,' said Farmer John, 'she used to drink too much sherry, that's all.'

'That's not true,' said Wendy. 'My Aunt Jessie was a clairvoyant, she was in touch with the spirit world.'

'Huh,' said Farmer John, 'is that so? I still think it's all nonsense.' And he gave the fire a poke with his foot.

Just then there was a knock at the door. Farmer John looked at Wendy. 'You answer it,' he said, 'it could be a ghost!'

Wendy got up and went to the door but when she opened it there was no-one outside. 'How strange,' she said. 'Perhaps it was the wind.'

'Don't you think it might have been a ghost?' said Farmer John sarcastically.

'Of course not,' said Wendy. 'It's just a windy night, something must have blown against the door, that's all.'

'Oh, that's all right then,' said Farmer John. 'I was beginning to feel scared!'

Wendy shut the door. 'Do you want to play a game?' she said. 'What about Scrabble?'

'OK,' said Farmer John.

They set the board up and started to play. Farmer John looked at his letters. He had an S, a T, an O and an H. 'Now what can I make with these,' he muttered to himself. Wendy put down a G. 'Aha!' Farmer John put his letters down. 'GHOST!' he said triumphantly.

Wendy laughed. She put down an A, a U, an N and a T next to the H. 'HAUNT,' she said. 'We *are* having a spooky game, aren't we?'

Farmer John looked at his letters. 'I know,' he said, and he put down O, N, I, G, H, T under the T. 'GHOST HAUNT TONIGHT,' he said. 'Oh dear that's a bit freaky.'

Suddenly the lights went out.

Wendy screamed. 'Oh my goodness, what's going on?!'

'It must be a power cut,' said Farmer John. 'Stay there and I'll get the candles.' Farmer John groped his way to the kitchen and found the cupboard. He felt for the candles and the matches. He was just about to turn round when he felt a tap on the shoulder.

'AAHH!' He jumped a mile in the air and dropped everything on the floor.

'HA HA HA!' Wendy laughed. She was standing right behind him.

'You didn't think I was a ghost, did you?'

'No I didn't,' said Farmer John crossly. 'How was I supposed to know it was you?'

They lit the candles and sat in the gloom. The candles flickered, making weird shadows round the room.

'Well,' said Farmer John, 'if a ghost is going to go haunting, this is a good time to do it.'

'Don't,' said Wendy, 'you're making me feel nervous.'

'Have you heard the story about the *old* empty barn?' said Farmer John.

'No,' said Wendy, 'I don't want to.'

'There was nothing in it,' said Farmer John.

'Ho Ho Ho,' laughed Wendy.

They sat and watched the fire. 'I'm cold,' said Wendy.

'But we've got the fire going,' said Farmer John.

'I know, but I'm freezing,' shivered Wendy. 'Do you think there's a ghost in the room?'

Farmer John looked a bit worried. 'You don't think our house is haunted too,' he said. 'It might be Aunt Jessie's ghost!'

'Her ghost was friendly,' said Wendy. 'I hope it's hers. What's that noise?' There was a strange scraping sound coming from behind the settee.

'That's creepy,' said Farmer John. 'What could it be?'

'I don't know,' said Wendy, 'probably just mice.'

The noise stopped.

'Hmm,' said Farmer John. 'I'm not so sure. What can we do now? It's too early to go to bed.'

'Let's sing songs,' said Wendy, 'to keep our spirits up.'

'Don't talk about spirits,' said Farmer John, 'you're giving me the creeps!'

'I was only trying to help,' said Wendy. 'Why don't we play a game?'

'We've already played Scrabble and look where that's got us,' said Farmer John.

'Let's play I spy, then,' said Wendy. 'I spy with my little eye something beginning with G.'

'GHOST!' said Farmer John. 'Where?'

'Behind you,' said Wendy. Farmer John jumped out of his seat.

Wendy hooted with laughter. 'You're as nervous as a kitten!'

'I suppose you think that was funny,' said Farmer John. 'I'm not scared.'

'Ssh,' said Wendy. 'Listen!'

There was a soft tap tap tapping at the window. Farmer John looked at Wendy. Wendy looked at Farmer John.

'I don't like that,' said Farmer John. 'Whatever could it be?'

'I dread to think,' said Wendy. 'Are you going to go and find out?'

'I don't like to,' said Farmer John.

'But I thought you said you weren't afraid of ghosts,' said Wendy.

'I'm not,' said Farmer John, 'I'm just a bit cautious, that's all.'

He carefully got up and tiptoed to the window. He peeped through the crack in the curtains, his heart was pounding. Then he gave a tremendous shout and flung the curtains wide open. 'HA!' he cried. 'Look, it's all the animals.'

Daisy the dairy cow, Mavis the ewe and Suzie the sow were standing outside. Farmer John opened the window. 'Hello you lot,' he said. 'What can I do for *you*?'

'Please John,' said Mavis, 'can we come inside? It's frightening out here. Daisy's been telling us all ghost stories and now we can't sleep.'

Farmer John laughed. 'Of course you can,' he said. 'Come in, the more the merrier.'

Daisy, Suzie and Mavis joined Farmer John in the sitting room and Farmer John made room for them by the fire. 'It looks like we weren't the only ones to be scared,' he said to Wendy, 'but there's safety in numbers. No ghost will bother us now while we're all together like this.'

Farmer John put another log on the fire. 'Now then, Daisy, what about a story?'

Daisy began. 'It was a *dark* and stormy night…and the brigands were gathered together… and the captain said to Antonio, 'Tell us a story' and Antonio began, 'It was a *dark* and stormy night…'

The wind howled outside, the fire crackled and rain pattered against the window-panes. One by one their heads began to nod, their eyes closed and it wasn't long before they were all sound asleep.

FARMER JOHN'S SECRET

All Wendy's beauty products begin to go missing. What can Farmer John be doing with them?

It was breakfast time on Thistledown Farm and Farmer John was munching his toast with the farming paper propped up against the marmalade jar.

'It says here,' he said to Wendy his wife, 'that there's a sheep show and sale next week at Dexeter market. I think I ought to enter Mavis for the show, she's the most beautiful sheep on the farm.'

Wendy laughed.

'You and your sheep,' she said. 'Anyone would think you loved them more than me!'

Farmer John smiled.

'Don't be silly,' he said. 'If I had to choose between you and my sheep I'd choose you every time.'

'Really?' said Wendy. 'You spend more time with your sheep than you do with me and I do believe you dream about them too.'

Farmer John laughed. 'Perhaps you're right,' he said, 'but you know I only keep them so I can look after *you*, my dear.'

'Hmm,' said Wendy, 'I'm not so sure, you never talk about anything else. It's 'my sheep this' and 'my sheep that', I'm beginning to feel a bit jealous.'

'Don't be ridiculous!' said Farmer John. 'How could anyone be jealous of a sheep? Now, I'm just popping out to go and see Mavis about that show.' And he put on his boots and cap and went up to the sheep shed.

Mavis the ewe was chewing some hay when he arrived.

'Morning, Mavis,' said Farmer John cheerily, 'how are you today?'

'Baa,' said Mavis, 'not baad, and yourself?'

'Oh, I'm OK,' said Farmer John, 'but I think Wendy is feeling a bit jealous.'

'Oh dear,' said Mavis. 'Why?'

'Well, it's because I'm always spending so much time with you,' said Farmer John, 'but never mind, it's only a phase she's going through.'

'Now look,' said Farmer John, 'there's a sheep show at Dexeter market and I want you to enter. We've got a few days to get ready, do you feel like doing it?'

'Oh yes,' said Mavis. 'I'm the most beautiful sheep on the farm, I'm bound to win.'

'Good,' said Farmer John. 'I knew you'd want to. Now, I have a few ideas that might interest you about *how* you might win…'

That night, when Farmer John went to bed, he asked Wendy if he could borrow her hairdryer.

'My hairdryer?' said Wendy. 'What on earth do you want with my hairdryer, you've got no hair to dry!'

'It's a secret,' said Farmer John. 'I can't tell you.'

Wendy laughed.

'Oh all right,' she said, 'but I'll want it back, don't go getting it all mucky.'

So next morning Farmer John took Wendy's hairdryer and went out.

He came back at lunchtime and gobbled down his food.

'That was nice,' he said, 'what was it?'

Wendy frowned. 'Well! I go to all the trouble of making a nice meal and you don't even notice what it was! What a nerve!'

'I'm sorry,' said Farmer John, 'but I was thinking about my sheep.'

'I might have guessed!' fumed Wendy. 'Don't bother asking for pudding because there isn't any.'

'Oh, OK,' said Farmer John. 'Can I borrow your curling tongs?'

Wendy looked astonished. 'What *are* you up to?' she said. 'All right, if you must but mind you look after them.'

Farmer John took the curling tongs and went out. He came back at tea-time looking very pleased with himself.

'Pooh,' said Wendy, 'you stink of sheep! What *have* you been doing?'

'That's for me to know and you to find out,' said Farmer John mysteriously.

Next morning Wendy asked Farmer John if he had seen her perfume.

'I don't think so,' said Farmer John. 'Where did you see it last?'

'Here on my dressing table,' said Wendy. 'I'm sure it was here yesterday.'

'I dunno,' said Farmer John, 'perhaps you put it somewhere else', and he went out to feed his animals.

Daisy was standing in the yard after milking.

'Moo,' she said, 'I hear you're entering Mavis in the sheep show, John.'

'Yes,' said Farmer John, 'she's the most beautiful sheep on the farm, she's bound to win.'

'That's as may be,' said Daisy, 'but there are lots of beautiful sheep around. You'll need to be lucky if Mavis is to win a prize.'

'Aha,' said Farmer John, 'I have a cunning plan.'

'What's that then?' said Daisy.

'It's a secret,' said Farmer John. 'You'll find out soon enough.'

When Farmer John came in for lunch Wendy asked him if he'd seen her nail varnish and lipstick. Farmer John looked surprised.

'Now what would I want with your nail varnish and lipstick?' he said.

'I don't know,' said Wendy, 'I can't find them anywhere.'

'Perhaps they're down the back of the sofa,' said Farmer John helpfully, and he gobbled down his lunch and went out.

Wendy was getting a bit fed up. She went to look for her scissors but she couldn't find them either. 'Where are all my things going?' she asked herself. 'There must be an explanation.'

Then she remembered that Farmer John had borrowed her curling tongs and hairdryer. She began to get a bit suspicious.

'That farmer's up to something,' she said. 'He's spending all his time with his sheep. I'm going to find out what's going on!'

She put on her coat and slammed the door. She marched up across the yard to the sheep shed. Farmer John was bending over a sheep in the corner.

'Now hold steady, Mavis,' he was saying, 'this won't take a moment...'

Wendy gasped. 'JOHN STUBBLEFIELD!' she cried. 'What *have* you been up to? How dare you take my make-up for your sheep!'

Farmer John jumped and dropped the lipstick. He had painted a bright red smile on Mavis's lips. She was wearing Wendy's false eyelashes, her wool was in curls and her toenails were painted with pink nail varnish!

Farmer John looked very guilty.

'I was only trying to make my sheep look pretty for the show, my dear,' he said.

'Don't you 'my dear' me!' said Wendy crossly, 'I knew you loved your sheep more than me and this proves it!'

'But Wendy,' cried Farmer John, 'I was only doing it for *you*. If Mavis wins a prize, I get £100 and then I can take you out for a special meal.'

'Is that true?' said Wendy. 'A special meal?'

'Yes,' said Farmer John. 'I haven't taken you out for ages, I meant it as a surprise.'

'Oh, John,' said Wendy, 'I'm so sorry!'

Farmer John gave Wendy a huge hug. 'Never mind,' he said, 'we'll go out another time.'

'No,' said Wendy. 'Mavis must enter the show, especially since you've made her look so beautiful.'

So Mavis entered the sheep show and won, and Farmer John paid for a table for two at a very smart restaurant. They had candles and soft music and it was highly romantic. Farmer John was extremely happy and Wendy enjoyed it very much and from then on she never worried about Farmer John spending so much time with his sheep again.